Going Hard

Jayne Rylon

eBook ISBN: 978-1-941785-13-3
Print ISBN: 978-1-941785-16-4

Edited By Mackenzie Walton
Cover Art By Jayne Rylon
Interior Print Book Design By Jayne Rylon

OTHER BOOKS BY JAYNE RYLON

DIVEMASTERS
Going Down
Going Deep
Going Hard

MEN IN BLUE
Night is Darkest
Razor's Edge
Mistress's Master
Spread Your Wings
Wounded Hearts
Bound For You

POWERTOOLS
Kate's Crew
Morgan's Surprise
Kayla's Gift
Devon's Pair
Nailed to the Wall
Hammer it Home

HOTRODS
King Cobra
Mustang Sally
Super Nova
Rebel on the Run
Swinger Style
Barracuda's Heart

Touch of Amber
Long Time Coming

Compass Brothers

Northern Exposure
Southern Comfort
Eastern Ambitions
Western Ties

Compass Girls

Winter's Thaw
Hope Springs
Summer Fling
Falling Softly

Play Doctor

Dream Machine
Healing Touch

Standalones

4-Ever Theirs
Nice & Naughty
Where There's Smoke
Report For Booty

Racing For Love

Driven
Shifting Gears

Red Light

Through My Window
Star

Can't Buy Love
Free For All

Paranormals
Picture Perfect
Reborn

Pick Your Pleasures
Pick Your Pleasure
Pick Your Pleasure 2

DEDICATION

For everyone who wishes they could travel more.

ONE

Tosin Ellis braced himself against the railing on the uppermost deck of the *Divemaster* megayacht. He tipped his face toward the breeze then drew fresh island air into his lungs until they threatened to pop. He loved the salty tang of the ocean, always would. Yet something about that first scent of earth after weeks surrounded by the sea overpowered his senses. Ripe with flowers and vegetation and rich dirt, it smelled like coming home.

In fact, after a long passage—like the nearly four thousand miles they'd just finished cruising from Midway Island, west of Hawaii, to the Cook Islands, in the BFE neighborhood of the South Pacific—his nose told them land was near before they spotted it on the horizon.

Well, his nose and Captain Alex's trusty GPS, along with the rest of the technology onboard. The bridge of the ship looked like it could easily transport them to Mars and back. Crossing a remote stretch of ocean...*pfft*. No problem.

An approaching boat carrying a welcoming committee drew his attention away from the green lump of Rarotonga on the horizon. The sense of rightness that accompanied the first indications of an approaching shoreline reminded him that although he spent a large portion of his life below the waves, guiding SCUBA divers through a marine paradise, he hadn't yet grown gills or evolved into a merman.

His new life goal.

Hey, he had to dream up something even wilder and crazier to aspire to than "multimillionaire", since Archer Banks had already helped him check that off his bucket list. He shook his head then rubbed his thumbs over the polished wood beneath them. The idea that he co-owned the *Divemaster*, a nearly three hundred foot luxury vessel, along with his two best friends still didn't seem quite real.

It had been about a year since Archer had inherited his father's billions and transformed himself, Tosin, and Miguel from perpetual beach bums into benevolent cruisers who invited deserving people on all-expenses-paid vacations of a lifetime. Together, they made sure their visitors had a great experience while they explored whatever corner of the world the ship happened to occupy at that moment. Maybe someday Tosin would accept that he wasn't dreaming.

He figured he could live and work here forever without growing sick of it. Something he'd never been able to say about a place or a job before.

Right then, though, he had visions of one thing he was lacking: a juicy cheeseburger.

The *Divemaster* had ridiculous amounts of storage compared to a typical yacht, but after the lavish meals the staff had prepared during their voyage, even she had grown light. It took a lot to feed the crew, the owners, and their guests for so long. Especially to their chef's standards.

Gone were the days of munching a granola bar or a banana for breakfast on his way to some backwoods dive shop. No, the kitchen staff insisted that everyone involved in the Divemaster Project ate well. And he wasn't complaining.

Tosin had enjoyed many delicious fresh fish dinners in a row. Some of which he'd contributed to himself through the bounty of his late afternoon deep sea fishing sessions. Still, he couldn't wait to sink his teeth into a hunk of low-grade, greasy ground beef.

If he was lucky, maybe he'd also find some female company to liven up a shared meal. Someone adventurous, willing to join him for a late-night private party in the ship's naughtily appointed clubroom afterward, would be even better.

Tosin observed as Captain Alex coordinated with the local harbormaster to position them as close as safely possible to the island before dropping anchor in a spot that wouldn't damage the reef encircling the volcanic island.

They didn't have facilities to accommodate a ship as large as the *Divemaster* within the ring of coral that formed a protective barrier between the open ocean and the beachside villages of Rarotonga. So they'd anchor out here and take tenders into Avatiu Harbour.

He should probably figure out where he'd stowed his flip-flops last time he'd come onboard, and scrounge around for a shirt. Maybe even one with buttons. Most of the time—when he wasn't suited up in dive gear—he roamed around in only his swim trunks. Or less.

It felt weird to wear actual clothes anymore. Still, he'd attempt to look halfway civilized when they stumbled onto these foreign shores, trying to find their land legs again.

Despite their inflated bank accounts, Tosin, Miguel, and Archer couldn't claim to have gotten much more sophisticated than they'd been when they roamed the globe, hopping from place to place whenever the whim arose and they could afford plane tickets to the next destination. Not so different from what they still did, except now they took their very fancy house with them when they moved.

Enjoying the perks of their newfound fortune, and sharing joy with as many other people as possible, held far more value to them than appearances.

With that said, his two best friends had somehow managed to snag a pair of the hottest, toughest, smartest women he'd ever met. More miraculously, it had nothing to do with their wealth. Their constant kissy faces, shared intimacy, and genuine affection were starting to make Tosin think he might have to change his greatest ambition from becoming Aquaman into something slightly more...*domestic*.

Otherwise he'd end up kicking it with Captain Alex and Banks—the manager of the Divemaster Project and the larger Banks Foundation, which consisted of the rest of Archer's charitable holdings— when he'd reached the confirmed bachelor stage in another decade or so. Not a terrible club to join if it came to that, he thought. Those two were pretty badass dudes.

Worse things could happen.

He should know, since trouble had accompanied their influx of cash. They'd pulled together to survive some hairy situations. Hopefully the crazy shit—you know, like murders, kidnappings, heists, and the rest of that ridiculous stuff—was behind them so they could simply relax from now on.

Out here, surrounded by a whole lot of not much for miles and miles and miles, Tosin was looking forward to some good old-fashioned sunning himself on the beach, dancing and drinking the night away, and maybe a hook up or two minus any drama.

Plus diving. Always diving.

The Cook Islands had some unique features he couldn't wait to investigate, starting with the lagoon between the shore and the barrier reef. It was like one giant aquatic playground. The cerulean water he could now see clearly contrasted with the darker midnight of the deeper ocean beating against the coral. It couldn't be more than ten feet deep in most places. It would be warm and teeming with sea life.

His version of paradise, for sure.

Overhead, the *whop whop whop* of a sleek helicopter taking off from the other side of the ship quickly faded as the transport zipped toward the verdant mountain that rose above the palm-dotted shore. He wished he'd planned ahead enough to grab a ride with Waverly, Archer's girlfriend, who would be flying the staff over to start their provisioning runs.

Less than a minute later, Archer trotted toward Tosin as if his thoughts had summoned the guy. Miguel trailed behind, joining them on the deck as the ship settled into its anchorage and the shore tenders were prepared. Time to go.

"You heading into town?" Archer asked as he chucked a white linen shirt and Tosin's shoes at his head.

He caught them with hardly any effort then nodded as he put them on. "It's probably too much to hope they have a Five Guys, huh?"

It certainly didn't look like a commercial sort of place from where he was standing. Large buildings or shopping malls didn't exist here. Hell, they'd be lucky to find a supermarket. He didn't truly mind, but he was serious about scoring some food.

Miguel snorted. He rubbed his flat stomach. "Yeah, but I could hit up a restaurant. You in?"

He looked to Archer, who cleared his throat before asking, "Could we make a pit stop first? While Waverly is busy helping the crew restock in the chopper, I thought we could check out the Punanga Nui Market. I hear they have a couple world renowned artists who sell their stuff there."

"Who'd you hear that from?" Tosin narrowed his eyes as his friend didn't quite meet his gaze. The Cooks were remote. Hardly anyone they knew had come here before and it certainly wasn't something he could ever remember talking about with travelers they'd run into along the way.

"Google," Archer admitted below his breath.

"You were looking up art galleries? Since when are you into that, Archie?" Miguel wondered.

Sure, the guy was technically a billionaire. He lived frugally, megayacht aside. They appreciated the beauty of nature above all else. The female form especially. Tosin would bet Archer couldn't name any more fine artists than he could. Van Gogh, Picasso, Michelangelo, the basics.

"I thought *Waverly* might be into it. I—uh, want to surprise her. If something catches my eye, I mean. I'll know it when I see it." Archer turned away then motioned for them to hurry. "You coming or not? Let's go."

Tosin looked over at Miguel, who shrugged then said, "I've got nothing to do for a while anyway. Sabine is taking advantage of the better internet connectivity here to transmit her test results and hold a few videoconferences. Besides, we'll probably stumble across someplace to eat along the way."

"Sounds good." Tosin strode side by side with his friend as they both studied Archer, who hustled to the tenders as if he needed to reserve a spot on his own damn boats.

What was up with that?

⌇ TWO ⌇

osin and Miguel continued to tease Archer about his unusual desire to shop as they skipped across some pretty gnarly waves. The island grew as they approached. The peak at its center loomed overhead. Blanketed with thick foliage, the craggy core of Rarotonga was obviously uninhabitable, which pushed its relatively small population of thirteen thousand people out into a ring around its edges.

Everything seemed supersaturated in the tropical sunlight. The bright sapphire of the water and the emerald of the trees were soon outdone by the scarlet birds fluttering around neon pink and yellow flowers they spotted as they tied up to the town dock. Used to the astounding hues of the underwater world, Tosin thought this might be one of the few places on Earth that could come close to mimicking its splendor. It was almost like when his sunglasses got smudgy and he cleaned them. Suddenly everything around him was crisp and clear and hyper-detailed.

"The market isn't far." Archer ignored their snickers and took off, marching down the street in the direction he'd pointed.

Miguel and Tosin exchanged a quizzical glance then followed at a stroll, taking more time to appreciate the landscape than their friend had. They traveled the length of the small town in only a few minutes before a cluster of tents, carts, and tables came into view.

Tosin sniffed the air as the scent of something sweet and coconut-y reached his nose. Miguel hummed and checked out a street vendor, buying a crispy stick of fried dough covered in what looked like cinnamon sugar. That would do for starters.

Tosin reached over and snagged the end of it, breaking it in half. "Thanks."

"Asshole," Miguel grumbled, though he laughed. "It's not like I wouldn't have shared it with you anyway."

"I know. But that was more fun." Tosin grinned as he chomped down on the treat. Flavor exploded in his mouth, making him eye Miguel's half enviously.

"Oh no. Go get your own if you want more." Miguel snarfed his portion in a couple of large bites, probably to make sure Tosin didn't steal any more of it. Wise move.

Up ahead, Archer turned back, glowering when he realized they'd been distracted by junk food. Not that that should come as a surprise to him. He waved them closer then ducked under a pretty purple and gold awning that held a very tidy array of jewelry.

Tosin peeled his gaze from ornate gardenia head wreaths, endless souvenirs, and the wooden Tangaroa carvings with giant dicks as he stepped inside just ahead of Miguel. He glanced up. When he saw the woman managing the stall, he nearly crashed into a display of long necklaces made of zillions of tiny pupu shells.

Only Miguel's fist at the back of his shirt helped steer him clear of disaster. His friend whispered, "Settle down, buddy, or you'll never have a shot. Better wipe those crumbs off your face, too."

Not the first impression Tosin would have liked to make.

He stepped fully into her booth, swiped his hand over his mouth to rid it of any stray sugar crystals or drool, then nudged his sunglasses lower on the bridge of his nose so that he could study the woman without heavy tint obscuring any of her beauty.

A white frangipani flower adorned her chestnut hair, which brushed the top of her perfect ass. A modified sarong—signs in other stalls they'd passed had called them pareu—wrapped her slender frame in a vibrant scarlet fabric with bold lime green leaf patterns.

Her rich skin tone reminded him of the oiled teak that dominated the interior of the *Divemaster*. It made his fingers itch to touch her. The exotic features of her striking face held an Asian flair made even more beautiful by her Māori ancestry. Lush lips and a bold nose kept her from appearing too delicate. He'd give her a solid seventeen on a scale from one to ten.

Despite her striking appearance, it was her smile that nearly burned out his retinas. Warm and welcoming, as pristine as the environment surrounding them, she could easily have been some Oceania goddess.

Immediately, he knew what he wanted to take home. Her.

Damn.

"Good afternoon. Can I help you?" She hadn't even noticed Tosin, her greeting aimed at Archer instead. That bastard.

Tosin attempted to focus by peering into the jewelry boxes propped on the tables around him instead of at her gorgeous face. Wow. It really was awesome. Everything he looked at called to him. Reminded him of the ocean and the wondrous things he admired beneath the surface. Carved shells, pearls of all hues, coral—she'd used a variety of nature's beauty to make her art.

"Are you Kahori Akama?" Archer asked.

Kahori. Tosin practiced saying her name a few times in his mind and decided he liked the way it sounded. Having an unusual name himself, he always appreciated someone else's.

How did Archer know of her? And why the fuck had he been holding out?

"I am." She held out a skilled hand—since it had presumably created the assortment of remarkable adornments surrounding them—to Archer.

Tosin didn't bother tamping down his jealousy when his supposed friend made contact with her.

"Nice to meet you. My name is Archer. I read the feature article about you in Australia's *Style Magazine.* It said you have a shop here on the island that showcases your more upscale creations," he explained to the pretty jeweler. "Is it open right now? I'm hoping I can take a look at some of your higher end pieces. I— uh—have my eye out for something special to give my girlfriend."

Tosin's head snapped to the side then as he finally pried his stare from Kahori. He met Miguel's knowing gaze. Things were starting to make sense.

Could Archer be looking for a *ring* for Waverly?

Miguel was grinning back at him. He must be thinking the same thing.

Kahori ignored their antics and dealt directly with Archer. "No, sorry. We're a small family-run business. My main operation is located on a smaller island north of here, Aituataki. It's where I grew up. I do have a gallery here, since Rarotonga draws the most tourists. But on market days we close up since my cousin and I are the only two clerks and we're both needed out here."

She gestured to the guy beside her that Tosin hadn't even noticed while his vision tunneled on her. The man was glaring at him. Probably because Tosin was scoping out the guy's family member as if she were the juicy cheeseburger he'd been hoping to devour earlier.

"I understand." Archer smiled.

Tosin could tell he was disappointed despite his graciousness. Sure, he could come back some other day, but he spent nearly all his time with Waverly and had taken a hard line approach against lying, even innocently, ever since a few misunderstandings and omissions had nearly wrecked the most important relationships in his life. Including his friendship with Tosin and Miguel. It wouldn't be easy for him to break away unnoticed in order to surprise her with his purchase.

"We'll keep Waverly busy if you want to sneak out and buy her a present another time." Tosin knocked his fist into Archer's shoulder. "What are friends for? I can't be responsible for how I distract her, though."

Archer practically snarled at that.

Kahori laughed then shook her head, setting the petals in her hair fluttering. "No need for violence, boys. The shop is just a block away. I'd be happy to take you over there for a quick look. You don't mind, do you, Hemi?"

She glanced over at her cousin, who did indeed seem put out. Or maybe he was just protective. Tosin could respect that. One gorgeous woman, three foreign men who looked like...well, them. Lots of expensive merchandise that they probably didn't seem able to afford. Yeah, he'd be bristling, too.

"I'll walk her home safe and sound when we're finished," Tosin promised.

"The islands aren't like that." Kahori rolled her eyes as if overwhelmed by too much testosterone. She patted her cousin on the shoulder. "This isn't some big city. It's fine. I'll be right back. I'll even bring you a beer."

The man nodded grudgingly at that. As they left the stall, he drew out his cell phone and spoke quietly to someone on the other end. Tosin figured they'd be supervised by Rarotongan natives the entire way.

He didn't mind.

But he did settle his sunglasses back into place so that it was less obvious that he was admiring the view from a few steps behind Kahori. She led Archer, Miguel, and Tosin as they proceeded down the street to her boutique.

Double damn.

∽ THREE ∾

Kahori acted as if she couldn't feel the tall blond foreigner watching her. The weight of his stare held a lot of impact, though. It bummed her out that she couldn't study him as intently as he seemed to be doing to her while she led him and his friends to her store.

It had been a long time since she'd been singed by the spark of attraction like the one he'd ignited when he'd stepped into her stall at the market. And it had been effortless on his part. The man hadn't spoken a single word to her. His impressively cut body and that self-depreciating smirk he'd flashed when he'd nearly trampled her display had been enough to do the trick. Her carefully practiced cool reserve had gone up in flames like deadwood smothered in lava.

Hopefully he couldn't tell how attracted she was to him on sight.

The easy friendship he shared with his almost-as-sexy companions, along with his unusual accent, had sealed the deal. She may not even have officially met the guy yet, but she already wished she could have bumped into him under different circumstances. In a different time. Before she'd vowed not to entangle herself in affairs that could only scar her further.

Which was precisely why she should continue pretending to ignore him. He could be dangerous to her and the walls she'd built to keep herself safe within them.

By the time she'd finished her self-lecture, she'd crossed the narrow road and drew her key from her clutch. Key. Singular. She didn't own a car and there was no need for locks on her home. If Rarotonga was tiny and remote, Aitutaki was ten times so. Everyone knew everyone. No one would dare steal from another resident. Heck, they were almost certainly related.

She opened the door and ushered the three men inside, shivering slightly when the blond man brushed up against her on his way inside. The doorway was no match for his broad shoulders. If she paused to savor the smell of him, sandalwood and spice, no one could blame her, right?

Shaking her head to clear the visions of what he might look like beneath that thin shirt from her mind, she focused on business. She couldn't let the opportunity for a sale slip through her fingers. It had been more than nine months since her last disastrous trip overseas and her savings were taking a hit. If she could put off leaving the security of her islands a while longer, she'd be grateful.

Kahori took a mental inventory, then asked, "So, what exactly is it you had in mind?"

"I'm looking for an engagement ring." Archer confirmed her suspicions.

The article he'd mentioned had highlighted her previous wedding sets. Unfortunately for him, that also meant she'd sold out of most of what she'd made. Though she'd recently completed a few new pieces, she hadn't brought them over to the store from her workshop yet. Mostly because they were more extravagant than what she typically sold here and had been hoping for an online buyer. Figured.

"I knew it!" The man with the South American accent whooped then high-fived Archer. The blond added a congratulatory slap on his back that would have rattled a normal person. Archer only beamed.

Kahori couldn't help herself. She grinned at his obvious devotion to his partner and the support his buddies gave him over his decision to commit himself to her. A wide network of friends her own age was something she missed out on growing up in the sparsely populated region. There had only been a couple dozen children around her age. Most of those had moved away in search of work on one of the surrounding islands or a higher standard of living and the modern amenities their homeland couldn't provide.

For a while, she'd thought that would be her fate, too.

Until she realized she couldn't cut it in the big, bad world.

Living in paradise had tons of benefits, and a few drawbacks she had learned to deal with. So she settled for vicariously enjoying her visitors' bond instead. When the guys had settled down, she opened the case that held her handmade rings. Most featured the very best pearls harvested from black-lipped oysters that she could source. The luster, orient, shape, color, size, and surface were each of the highest caliber. Thick layers of nacre provided plenty of aragonite crystals to reflect the light.

Considering the Cook Islands were the second largest source of black pearls, some of which she'd been lucky enough to collect herself, she had a decent selection even after she'd burned through a bunch.

Archer and his friends—she'd heard him call the dark-haired guy Miguel and the blond Tosin—leaned in, their heads nearly cracking together as they tried to fit their well-muscled bodies in the compact space. They complimented her designs. Their praise seemed genuine as they pointed out features they liked.

Warmth flooded her when Tosin peeked up at her and said, "I don't know shit about this, but everything I see is amazing. We're divemasters. This one here reminds me of a wave."

Which was exactly what she'd intended with the shell swirled in gold. Bonus, now she could imagine him in a skin-tight wetsuit, gliding beneath the surface of the ocean, one of her favorite pastimes.

Archer hummed. "They're all fantastic. Seriously. But..."

"It has to fit your girlfriend's personality." Kahori wasn't placating him. Especially for something as important as an engagement ring, it had to be just right. "Tell me about her."

"Waverly is unique. Strong. A helicopter pilot who served in the US Navy for almost a decade. She doesn't take shit from anyone and she's survived a lot of things that would have crushed other people." Archer's eyes went kind of glassy as he sang the praises of the woman he wanted to spend forever with. "She's brave, feminine, and..."

"Sexy as hell," Miguel added with a wink.

Kahori giggled, wishing she were half as awesome as Waverly. Especially the brave part. "She sounds fiery and bold. Special."

Archer nodded. "She is."

Kahori had the perfect thing. Except... "I'd like to show you something. Unfortunately, it's not here in the shop today. It's back in my workshop on Aitutaki. I only fly out here once a week for the market and I've never had someone come in looking for anything quite like this, so I've never brought it here. It's on my website, though. I can show you pictures."

"Sure, let me take a look." Archer smiled. "We're actually heading up that way in a few days, after we restock and refuel. Miguel and his girlfriend Sabine have a proposition for the island council regarding a business they'd like to establish in the area."

Kahori didn't burst their bubble by letting them know how reluctant some of the natives could be when it came to working with outsiders. They'd see themselves when they visited. Aitutaki made Rarotonga look like a bustling metropolis. What could they possible want with an area so secluded?

Not her problem at the moment.

"I should probably warn you." Kahori hesitated, scared of offending him but also afraid of springing the bad news on him too late, which could lead to an awkward conversation. "It's my most expensive piece."

"That's okay. I'd like to see it." Archer didn't hold her cautioning him against her.

"Great, let me bring it up on my laptop." She scooted around the counter and browsed to the ring's listing while the guys roamed the shop.

Miguel tapped the glass over a set of chandelier earrings dotted with baroque black pearls she favored for their unusual shapes and oil slick colors. "When you're done with Archer, I'll take these. They'll go great with Sabine's necklace."

Archer hummed. "Good eye."

"Just saying, I'm hoping to reserve the clubroom later. So time your gift wisely if you're hoping for a special thank you from her," Tosin mumbled to his friend.

Kahori had no idea what that meant. From his smoky tone and the flare of his friend's eyes, she could guess it was something scandalous, though. What would it be like to have a man like that worship her?

She shivered.

Meanwhile, Tosin paused and inspected the matching set of bracelets she'd tucked into the far corner of her display. Though they were for sale, she'd semi-consciously sabotaged them by hiding them behind other items. Kahori had been tempted to keep them for herself. But after her last trip abroad, she'd given up on the dream of finding someone to wear them with her and put them for sale. They were her favorite things she'd made, though by far not the most elegant or the priciest.

No, for that, she had to come back to Archer.

"Here it is." She spun the laptop around so he could see the screen. "It's a size five as is. I can adjust it as needed."

The man stood there, his mouth slightly open, and stared.

He blinked.

Didn't say a word.

Archer must hate it. She'd been so sure, though. Based on his description, it fit.

"What do you think, Tosin?" Archer asked, his voice kind of wispy and odd.

Except Tosin couldn't have an opinion. He hadn't so much as glanced at the computer or her crowning achievement. When Kahori flicked her gaze in his direction to assess his reaction, she realized he had removed his sunglasses and was staring at her again with the palest steel blue eyes she'd ever seen. "Stunning."

She blushed when Miguel snorted softly behind his hand. Then he peered over Archer's shoulder and whistled. "Wow. Now *that's* a ring."

Tosin did look then. He whipped his gaze to the picture then back at her in a dramatic double-take. His eyes grew wide as he scanned the purple-hued black pearl surrounded by a circle of alternating pear-shaped diamonds and fire opals, set in a lotus pattern around it. The fine band split into a Y on either side of the center. Perched on top, the embellishments appeared to hover over the finger of the wearer.

"You seriously made that?" he asked Kahori.

"I did." Pride bubbled up in her at the appreciation and awe he projected with his slightly tipped head and squinted eyes, as if he couldn't quite believe her capable of a feat that marvelous. To be frank, she'd blown herself away with this ring.

"What are you waiting for?" Miguel elbowed Archer.

The man raked his fingers through his short hair then scrubbed them over the stubble shadowing his cheeks and strong jaw. Then he asked his friends, "Am I doing the right thing?"

"By proposing? Hell yeah. Waverly is the woman for you," Miguel reassured him.

"No, I'm certain about that. Never have been more positive about anything in my life. But...the ring..."

Kahori understood his concerns. It was an unconventional selection. Not in the least bit traditional. Though she guessed his soon-to-be fiancée would approve, she only had the few scraps he'd shared with her about the woman to go on.

"Would you maybe just block your ears for a second? I think what I'm about to say might sound rude." Archer grimaced at her then turned to Miguel and Tosin. "Do you think Waverly will be into this instead of some honking rock? I could buy her a big ass diamond. I like this a million times better. It reminds me of something a mermaid queen would wear. But we're all about the ocean. Maybe she's not as into it..."

"Archie, quit worrying." Tosin put his hand on his friend's shoulder and squeezed. "Waverly is into *you*. That's the only thing she gives a fuck about. This ring is the bomb and she's going to freak out when you give it to her because, for some reason, she really loves you. Dumbass."

Kahori sighed behind the counter, her eyes going soft and melty at his passionate speech. If the men's friendship made her jealous, the fantasy of a soulmate like that...

Whew.

She fanned herself a few times while the guys talked amongst themselves.

"How are you going to pop the question by the way?" Miguel asked. "It's got to be something elaborate. A huge gesture, right? Something she'll never forget."

"I haven't thought that far ahead." Archer groaned. "Can't I just give it to her in bed after amazing sex and tell her how much I want to spend every night just like that?"

"No." Miguel and Tosin both caught her by surprise when they objected in unison.

"That doesn't sound half bad to me." She clapped her fingers over her mouth when she realized she'd spoken her thought out loud.

Tosin met her gaze and they chuckled together. The heat in his stare rivaled the sun beating down on the shop in its intensity. She wondered what it would be like to look into his eyes as he made love to her.

Whoa. No point in torturing herself with visions of something that would never happen.

"I'll worry about that later." Archer looked again at the picture of the ring, running the cursor over it as if he could stroke it through the screen. "How much is it?"

"Uh…" Kahori winced. "Remember, I told you—"

"I'm not surprised." Archer smiled. "Hit me."

She wrung her fingers, recalculating the cost of her materials. It was clear this ring had been destined for these people. It would make her happy for them to leave the Cook Islands with it. But she also liked to eat and pay her bills. Finding a middle ground, she gave Archer a discount without him knowing. "Fifteen thousand."

He didn't so much as flinch.

"Is that a fair price?" Archer asked her point blank.

She nibbled her lip before nodding.

"You're sure?" he asked again. "Look, I'm not even going to try to haggle with you. I don't know what I'm doing except appreciating something this beautiful. So I'm trusting you here. It's spectacular, and I think my girlfriend will love it. That's my only concern. If you tell me it's worth fifteen grand, I believe you."

"You're getting one hell of a deal," Kahori promised. "It's the best piece I've ever made. Easily worth what I've quoted you even if you smelted it and sold it for its components."

She grimaced then, pained to consider such a fate.

"Then why'd you hesitate?" Tosin asked. Nothing in his tone was accusatory. He seemed genuinely curious.

"Everything is relative, I suppose." She smiled softly then gave them a sliver of the truth. "You're here, the ring is here—well, nearby—and you're saving me a trip to Australia, New Zealand, China, or one of the bigger markets to find a buyer. I used to travel more often when I was establishing my brand. I just...prefer not to do that anymore if I don't have to. Now that my work is out in the world, gaining recognition, high-end buyers have been coming to me. Searching me out in person like you have or working with me remotely through my website on custom designs."

"Hang on..." Tosin interrupted her rambling as he realized where she was going. "You're saying you quoted Archer less than you would otherwise because you don't have travel expenses and time invested in unloading it?"

"Exactly." Kahori beamed. He blinked, as if her smile dazzled him far more than the jewels surrounding them did. "In one of those locations, the price would have been double."

Miguel slapped Archer on the back. "You'd better pony up. Don't want Waverly to think you cheaped out on her."

Kahori laughed.

Until she figured out that they weren't joking.

Archer held his card out to her in a flash. "Charge me for the full thirty-thousand, please."

She gawked, her stare winging between the three men as if they were about to spring some kind of trap.

Tosin intervened. "Trust me. He can afford it. Go ahead, *Kahori*."

The sound of her name rolling off his lips in his European accent was the best bonus she'd ever received. She hoped he couldn't see her pebbling nipples given the way she'd tied her pareu that morning, mimicking a strapless sundress.

"You're sure?" she asked Archer one final time.

"Absolutely." He waved toward the register. "Hurry before someone else comes along and swipes it out from under me."

Not likely. This single sale would be her biggest ever. It would cover her modest living expenses for several years. He was handing her what amounted to a fortune for some of her neighbors, who still practiced—and enjoyed—subsistence living. Though she was starting to get the feeling it was a drop in the bucket to these guys.

When the transaction was complete and Archer laid the pen next to his fresh signature on the receipt, she reached out and shook his hand. "Thank you so much. What size would you like the ring to be when you pick it up next week?"

Archer laughed. "I tried to get a few stealth measurements off other ones she has. I was going to go with a five anyway. Banks, a friend of ours, keeps rambling about fate lately. I'm starting to believe that old bastard might be on to something."

If that was true, did it mean she was destined to exist in solitude?

Was that what she'd learned on her disastrous voyage away from home? That she didn't belong anywhere else but here? Alone?

Kahori refused to let those shadows darken her mood. Not today, bad memories. Not today.

Before she could derail her own happiness, Miguel reminded her about the earrings he wanted as well. She wrapped them in pretty paper and a box, thinking about how on any other day it would have been a major sale. While she did that, Tosin pointed to the bracelets he'd noticed before.

"I can't be left out. How much for the masculine version of the leather, coral, and shell bracelet? This one, way in the back." He lifted his chin at his friends. "Unlike these guys, I'm single. Selfish, too. I want some of your work for myself."

"Oh." Kahori paused, trying to find a tactful way to decline. "I'd prefer not to separate the his-and-her set. They're carved from the same components. See how they fit together? It's actually my favorite thing I've ever made, though obviously not the finest."

Archer had clearly snagged that object for himself.

Kahori opened the back of the case and laid the bracelets beside each other. Tosin watched carefully as the organic curves tucked into each other and made a single shape when connected, sort of like a best friend charm girls gave each other.

"You're right. They belong together." He smiled at her, close enough as they leaned over the counter together that she could detect the flecks of silver mixed into his irises. Tosin inspired all sorts of ideas for creations in her mind. She wished she had a sketchbook right then. "I'll take them both, please."

Kahori trailed her finger over the familiar length of the bracelets in a loving goodbye before she packaged them as well. The day was easily the best in the history of her shop. And she had these three guys to thank for it.

When she handed Tosin the package, their fingers brushed. She sucked in her breath and tried not to drop the bag when he curled his hand around hers.

Tosin repaid her unintentional compliment. "I'm not going to lie. I expected to be bored out of my mind when Archie dragged us out shopping this afternoon. But you've made the experience extremely enjoyable."

"Thank you." She tried not to stammer when hit with the full blast of his charm. "I'm just doing what I love. Making unique, wearable art out of the beautiful things around me."

Way to sound like a commercial, Kahori.

"And doing it well. Since you seem to be a fan of uniqueness, and I'm willing to bet you've never met a person named Tosin before, maybe you should let me buy you dinner to celebrate today's success?" He rubbed his thumb lightly over her knuckles.

She laughed, wishing she could say yes. Desperate to keep from doing something foolish, she latched onto the obvious excuse. "Sorry, I really have to get back to the market. Hemi is probably losing his mind by now. He hates using the register app on his smartphone. Or technology in general, really. Or talking to strangers. And the daily commuter flight to Aitutatki leaves right after we pack up."

"Too bad." He released her hand by degrees, letting their fingers glide over each other almost reluctantly as he let her go.

Kahori sighed, deflating a little as the absence of the contact left her feeling hollow.

Instead of leaving it at that, Tosin tried once more, flattering her with his persistence. "Well then, how about when we pick up the ring in Aitutaki?"

"I'll think about it." She smiled softly then turned away to hand Archer her contact information.

When they'd made tentative plans for his pick up and exchanged thank-yous, she leaned against the doorframe. Free to stare, she greedily eyed Tosin until he disappeared around a corner, admiring the way he moved—sure and smooth. As much as she would like to learn more about the handsome stranger, she knew there was no way she'd accept his invitation.

Hopefully he'd forget all about it, and her, by the time he visited her hometown.

She should have realized he wouldn't.

∽ FOUR ∾

"**D**ude, from the amount of pacing and primping you've been doing this morning, I'd almost think you were the one picking up an engagement ring today," Miguel grumbled at Tosin. "Sit your ass down. You're making me jumpy."

Archer, on the other hand, relaxed on a lounger beside Banks. The older guy patted Archer's shoulder and smiled. "I've waited a long time to see your ring on Waverly's finger. You did well, kid."

"Guys, she hasn't said yes yet." Archer did seem to tense then. Not only because he was peering around to make sure his girlfriend didn't hear their conversation and blow his cover, either.

Miguel, Tosin, and Banks only cracked up.

"What's so funny?" Captain Alex asked as he joined them on the deck.

"Archie's worried Waverly might turn down his proposal." Banks shook his head ruefully.

"Don't be an idiot, boss." Captain Alex laughed too. "That woman loves you more than I love this ship. And that's a hell of a lot." Then he turned to Miguel and said, "So...are you really going to let him show you up like that?"

"What do you mean?" the divemaster asked, crossing his arms. They were competitive if nothing else.

"He wants to know when you're going to man up and commit to Sabine." Tosin enjoyed turning the tables on his friend. Take that, asshole.

Miguel blinked. "I—uh—I mean, you know, I already *am* committed. At least I have a girlfriend, unlike you. It's just that this doesn't seem like a good time. She's completely engrossed in her study and has so many other more important things going on right now. Or at least that's what I figured. Am I messing this all up again?"

Now the guys laughed at him. It was fun to see him squirm.

Except Banks let him off the hook. "You know what's best for the pair of you. It's clear that you love her. Don't rush if you're not ready. Either of you. Plus, Marta will be visiting soon—"

"Don't you know the exact number of hours until she touches down with the next batch of guests?" Tosin teased. No one was exempt from their ribbing around here. Banks had shown definite interest in Miguel's girlfriend's quasi-mom. At this point it was clear the woman was visiting to see *two* people, not just one.

"One hundred and twenty seven," Banks confirmed with a wink. "Anyway, since she's the closest thing to family Sabine has left, I'd recommend you do the gentlemanly thing and speak to her about it first while she's onboard if you think it's something you might pursue down the road."

"If you let Marta out of your cabin, you mean?" Captain Alex joked this time.

"Precisely." Banks flashed a sinful grin that proved beneath his proper exterior he had a wicked streak at least as wide as any of the divemasters'.

Poor Marta wasn't going to know what hit her. Or maybe she already had a clue since she and Banks had been videochatting—or exchanging emails when the connection speed didn't permit screen-to-screen conversations—pretty much every night for the past six months or so.

Miguel swallowed hard. "I'll talk to Kahori about sketching something up while we're there. I don't have to give it to Sabine until the time is right. *Right*?"

Captain Alex slapped him on the back. "Smarter every day. Anyway, I came out here to tell you lazy fools we'll be anchored and ready to go ashore in about ten minutes. I'd better see to that."

Tosin could make out Maunga Pu, the highest point on Aitutaki, barely four hundred feet above sea level. They really were close. If it wouldn't have taken him longer to swim than to wait for Captain Alex to park the *Divemaster*, he would have gladly launched himself over the rail and torpedoed toward the crystalline beaches along the shore.

It had only been a few days since his run in with Kahori, but he hadn't been able to think of much else beside her smile. And the things he'd like to do to her to guarantee he'd see more of it. Of her in general.

In addition to their appointment with her, the guys had a busy day planned. They'd set up a meeting with the village council in Aruntanga, the main town on the island, to pitch a grow dome for the medicinal algae Sabine and Miguel had discovered, which gave every indication it would be the central component in a cure for cancer that could eliminate deaths from the disease in their lifetime.

The Banks Foundation would fund the initiative and provide jobs along with income to any residents willing to work on the project. They could drastically improve the entire economy of the Cook Islands if the residents would allow it. Tourism, offshore banking, pearls, and fish exports lumped together couldn't do as much for them as involvement in the biomedical industry could.

To help prove they had only the best of intentions, they'd also arranged to sponsor an "island night", which Tosin understood was the Cook Islands' equivalent of a Hawaiian luau. There was only one woman on the entire island he would beg to accompany him to the celebration of local culture, complete with traditional music, dancing, and a literal boatload of food.

He would gladly beg if it came to that.

The first thing he'd done when they'd gotten back to the *Divemaster* after their shopping trip earlier in the week was steal the magazine Archer had discovered Kahori in. Tosin may or may not have clipped out the story and stashed it in his nightstand drawer after reading it a dozen times.

The interview about her commitment to her art and her connection to nature's beauty had only made him want to find out more about her. They had a lot in common. A passion for ocean conservation, for one. Diving, for another.

Kahori had named SCUBA as her favorite recreational activity.

Only really fantastic sex surpassed diving in Tosin's estimation.

He would happily enjoy some of both with her. If she'd only give him a shot. The *Divemaster* could be in the area for a while if the village council gave them the green light. He was looking forward to spending as much of that time as possible with Kahori.

Would she be down with that?

It seemed like at least as long as it had taken them to cross the Pacific, but was really probably less than an hour, before Tosin strode toward Kahori's main workshop, located in her house. He tried not to crush the bouquet he'd bought from a vendor at the dock as he kept up with Archer's absurd pace.

"You two are killing me," Miguel laughed, not at all winded but highly amused at their eagerness.

Neither Tosin nor Archer gave a shit. They were men on missions.

Archer consulted the crude map someone had drawn for him. There were no street names or house numbers to reference. They'd followed more basic directions, turning at the yellow cottage then following the cracked stone pathway for about a quarter of a mile when a stucco bungalow with a thatched palm roof came into view. Sea glass and shells dangled from ribbons, making the entire porch sparkle. They also acted as a privacy screen that still allowed some light to pass through. Between the strands, Tosin spied an underwater mural, which covered the back wall of the outdoor space, setting him immediately at ease.

He didn't need a GPS to know this was where Kahori lived and worked.

Two men sat on a bench beside the front door as if guarding the home. From them?

Tosin tried to put them at ease when he recognized the younger of the pair. "Hey there, Hemi. How's it going?"

The guy only grunted in response. An older, tanner, grumpier version of the dude crossed his arms over a massive chest that did his Pacific Islander ancestors proud. Legit tribal tattoos covered a portion of his face in an inked mask. More designs covered his right shoulder and half of his torso. Intricately carved bone earrings pierced his lobes. Fierce and proud, he looked like he could rip someone in half with his bare hands if he chose.

"We're here to pick up a ring from Kahori." Archer tried to be civil, too.

"Ms. Akama, *my daughter*, will be with you soon. You're early."

Tosin noticed the man didn't offer them his name or a seat for that matter. Though he did glare at the flowers Tosin now attempted to shield behind his body. Miguel disguised his chuckle with a cough.

A solid five awkward minutes passed before Kahori appeared at the door. "Pāpā, when they get here, show them to my studio?"

Tosin cleared his throat and she jumped a little. "Oh! I'm so sorry. I didn't realize you were here. I hope you weren't waiting long."

"Not at all." Miguel shrugged, as if they'd spent the time with her relatives in engaging conversation instead of a staring match.

"Nice to meet you, Mr. Akama." Tosin figured it couldn't hurt to be nice. Maybe later his kindness would ensure he'd simply receive a stern lecture for ogling the man's daughter instead of the ass-kicking he probably deserved for the things he'd like to do with her.

Definitely *not* dad-approved activities.

"Sorry. He's not used to outsiders." Kahori winced at the term, probably the most polite way of putting it she could. "Okay, that's not quite true. My uncle owns the resort on the lagoon. *Pāpā* chooses to keep to himself and the people he grew up with instead of expanding his horizons."

"No one knows better than me that you can't dictate how your family acts." Archer attempted to put her at ease. "Don't sweat it."

Maybe things here were going to be more difficult for Sabine and her scientific crew than they'd anticipated. If too many of the residents felt like Kahori's dad, they might not be setting up shop here after all.

Miguel poked Tosin between the shoulders, hard.

When Tosin snapped out of his thoughts, he realized Kahori was staring at him and the flowers he clutched. "Hello again. These are for you."

He held them out to her and watched her eyes grow wide, as if no one had ever given her a bouquet before.

"They're beautiful. Thank you." She treated him to her full-on smile as she accepted them then spun to put them in one of the pretty glass jars that decorated the her windowsill before filling it with water.

Kahori leaned in and drew a deep breath, savoring their fragrance before lifting her gaze to his. When Miguel shuffled in the corner, the spell broke. She set the flowers down then wiped her hands on her pareu, which was tied in a halter-style today.

The vibrant colors and conforming fabric highlighted her killer body.

"Sorry. My studio is this way. Come. I can't wait for you to see the ring in person." She spoke to Archer then, as if ashamed for taking a moment for herself before conducting business. Maybe tonight, at the festival, she'd be more relaxed.

Tosin could stand to wait a little longer to have her to himself.

She was interested, he could tell. The rest he could figure out.

Soon any thoughts beside praise for her craftsmanship flew out of his brain. He studied her workspace—along with the jewelry in progress on every flat surface—before taking a look at Waverly's ring.

Holy hell. Miguel was screwed. Tosin couldn't imagine the guy coming up with something equally impressive for Sabine, though several of Kahori's other creations also blew him away.

"Thank you again." Archer practically groveled at her feet as they collected the box and prepared to leave. "I can't wait to introduce you to Waverly tonight. It's going to be hard to pretend like we don't already know you, though. I hate lying. Especially to her."

"I think it's okay in these circumstances," Kahori laughed. "Though now that you mention it, I hope I don't spoil the surprise either."

"So you're coming then?" Tosin double-checked. "I had hoped I might get to share a meal with you after all. Or maybe you could be my tutor on the cultural program for the evening."

And maybe after that, he could teach her a little about how he rolled too.

"Of course. Practically the entire island will be there. At least to grab a bite to eat, if not to socialize.

Fewer than two-thousand people live on Aitutaki," she told them.

"Then it's a date?" he asked.

Right about the time her father ambled into the room. He huffed, then growled, "Kahori should focus on business tonight. The pearl traders will all be in from their posts. It's a good time to make deals."

"One night off won't hurt, *Pāpā*." Kahori softened her father's rough edges. "Besides, I already told Tuiara that I would perform. So you'll get to see me doing some of our traditional dances."

Tosin didn't care if her dad was right there and the size of a refrigerator. He nearly did a jig himself.

Night made.

His time in other South Pacific countries made him pretty damn sure this was going to involve a lot of hip shaking and bared skin. Count him in. "I'll make sure to sit in the front row then."

Her father took a step toward him.

Miguel intervened to keep Tosin's teeth firmly attached to his skull. "We'll stop interrupting you now so that you can enjoy tonight, then. If you have some availability in the next couple of days, maybe I could come back to discuss commissioning another ring from you. One for *my* girlfriend this time."

Kahori's father backed off a little at the promise of more profits. The three divemasters drifted out to the porch, leaving him to smolder in peace in her workshop. She glanced over her shoulder to make sure he hadn't followed.

"Thanks again for the flowers. See you tonight," Kahori said quietly to Tosin before rushing to close the gap between them. She went onto her tiptoes, braced her hands on his shoulders, and kissed his cheek before spinning away fast enough that he couldn't capitalize on the moment to forge a deeper connection. Her pareu flapped around her shapely thighs as she disappeared into her studio.

"*Pāpā*, I can't believe you were so rude," he heard her hiss. "They're good customers. And...just...good people."

"No *papa'a* is good enough for you. If you're finally interested in having a boyfriend, there are a half dozen local boys who are interested in the position," her father snapped in response without even trying to disguise his objection from the men outside. "Now, where are the boxes for today's shipment? If they're ready, I'll deliver them to the airport for you."

Tosin made sure they were well away from her cottage and out of sight of any prying eyes before he high-fived his friends. It may not have gone as smoothly as he'd hoped, but he was making progress.

Tonight was going to be epic.

∽ FIVE ∾

Kahori could have kicked herself for giving in to her impulse earlier. Kissing Tosin had been reckless. Especially with her disapproving father in the room next door. She hadn't wanted Tosin to believe her as intolerant and impolite as her family, though. Especially not when he'd been so freaking nice to her. And—okay, she admitted it— when everything about him turned her on.

Maybe indulging her lust with him would be the safest sort of affair.

After all, it wouldn't be long before he was waving *bon voyage* from the ridiculous yacht she'd heard he'd cruised up on with his friends. Given the way they'd dropped money without hesitation in her shop, she was beginning to wonder exactly who they were and what they were up to around these parts. They didn't seem like simple tourists.

Hopefully tonight she could find out more.

It couldn't hurt to get to know Tosin a little, could it?

Kahori took extra time lining her eyes and applying a stain made of crushed flowers and berries to her lips. She wove some of the blossoms Tosin had brought her into the length of her hair then shrugged into her traditional outfit. Every girl had a coconut bra or two in their closet, didn't they? If not, they should, because this one made her rack look pretty impressive.

She smiled into the mirror, humming as she tied her *kikau* around her waist. Over the grass skirt she fastened her most elaborate *titi*, which hugged her hips. The combination of feathers, shells, and dried fronds stood out from her midsection like a ballerina's tutu. It would accentuate the swing of her body to the beat of the drums. She'd made the costume herself, collecting only the most striking materials from the island around her until she was satisfied.

To her, the outfit was as much of a masterpiece as the ring she'd sold Archer.

Could Tosin be more appreciative of the unfamiliar than her own family? She hoped so.

Kahori didn't know how to make herself any more appealing than this. It had to be enough. Because although she hadn't intended to tangle herself up with him, the simple kiss she'd ambushed him with before hadn't quenched her desire for a taste of him.

She stared at herself in the mirror then adorned herself with wooden bracelets, pearl necklaces, and feather earrings from her collections until she was weighed down with a relative fortune in gorgeous things.

This was her turf. Tonight would be different than the last time she'd surrendered to curiosity about her sexual urges.

And if it ended badly, then at least her father would have the satisfaction of being right.

Kahori glanced at the clock, though she could already hear the sounds of drummers warming up on their *pates*. She had to hurry. Without bothering with shoes she'd only kick off when it came time to dance, or walk along the beach in the moonlight afterward, she set off down the dirt road that wound from her house to the village's gathering place, where island nights and other formal celebrations were held.

After she'd trekked nearly half the distance to town, she realized she'd forgotten the *poi*—weighted balls on chains wrapped in a slow-burning fuse—she needed for the *ura rama* fire dance. Cursing under her breath, praying she didn't ruin the effort she'd taken on her appearance, she trotted back toward home.

When she approached, it surprised her to see a glow coming from her studio. Had she forgotten to turn off the lights in her haste?

Get yourself together, Kahori!

She ripped herself over her forgetfulness and the way she'd absolutely lost her mind over a handsome man, who probably wouldn't turn out to be half as exciting or as good in bed as she had built him up in her mind to be.

Kahori charged inside, ready to grab her torches, and heard rummaging in the other room.

Someone was there!

"Hello?" she called.

"Kahori?" Hemi answered.

"Hey, did you need something? I'm late." She scooped up her torches, slipped the leather loops on their handles over her hands, and stuck her head in the other room.

"There were some packages that needed to go out this afternoon," Hemi reminded her.

"Oh, sorry. *Pāpā* took those to the airport office for me earlier. All except the one I haven't quite finished yet. I thought he would have mentioned it." Kahori hoped Hemi hadn't spent too long looking for them. "You coming?"

"Maybe later." He shrugged. "You look great, though."

"Thanks." She sighed in relief.

"That guy doesn't deserve one of our best." He shook his head as he mumbled then shut off the light, leaving with her, though they went in separate directions once they reached the street.

"Careful, Hemi, or you'll turn into my *Pāpā* soon." She rolled her eyes as she called over her shoulder to him. He shot her a vulgar gesture.

Kahori only laughed, then took off again, this time trotting as the rhythm of the drums rent the sultry evening air, calling her onward. She ran toward the savage pounding in time to the beat until she wasn't sure if the crashing of the sea on the barrier reef—the strongest force she'd ever experienced before—or the raging anticipation within her held greater power.

She was about to find out.

Please, let me be ready for the storm I am about to unleash.

SIX

Punctuality wasn't Tosin's strongpoint. Yet he'd dragged his friends to the island night celebration sickeningly early. He'd parked himself on a blanket right in the absolute center of the front row and refused to budge in case someone swiped his place. Delicious aromas wafting out of the *umukai*—an oven dug in the earth, filled with basalt rocks to hold in heat for slow roasting—as villagers unwrapped banana leaves from a feast of suckling pigs. Even those mouth-watering smells couldn't persuade him to abandon his spot.

Though it was making him hungry as hell.

"Waverly, if you love me you'll go grab me a snack to hold me over until after the performances." He flashed her his best imitation of baby seal eyes. "Please. I'm dying."

"Fine. Only because I think it's cute that you have such a crush on the girl who made Sabine's amazing earrings." She eyed the jewelry dangling from their friend's ears longingly, then patted his knee. "And because it smells so damn good I need to check it out for myself anyway."

Archer didn't need any prodding. He followed Waverly, and his stomach, toward the buffet that was being set up. Not before he flashed them a discreet yet enthusiastic thumbs-up. Tosin knew it was because his girlfriend had appreciated Kahori's artistry.

There was no doubt Waverly was going to adore the ring Archer had selected for her nearly as much as she loved the man himself.

That left Tosin wedged between Banks, who stretched out on his back, staring at the twilight sky, on one side of him and Sabine, who sat on Miguel's lap, on the other. "For the record, I do not have a *crush* on Kahori."

No, the things he had in mind had far less to do with puppy love and a whole lot more to do with very adult appetites.

"Probably for the best," Miguel said with a smirk. "Because if you did, you'd have to compete with every other dude between the ages of eighteen and sixty on this island for her attention."

Tosin followed his friend's gaze to the woman in question. She approached at a trot that set all his instant favorite parts of her body jiggling enticingly. Even Banks hummed. "That's her?"

"Yup." Tosin tried not to pant.

Worse, he clamped his mouth shut to keep from extolling her other virtues. Like how she'd been super insightful when helping Archer find the perfect ring. Or how she'd been honest and fair in setting her price despite Archer's disclaimer. Or how she'd advocated for the use of clean energy with logical strategies in her magazine interview. Or how she excelled at both creative and business pursuits, building her brand from the ground up while earning the appreciation of thousands of art connoisseurs around the world.

And yeah, she was gorgeous and inherently sensual on top of all those other things.

It wasn't often that Tosin's dick and his brain both appreciated the same woman. Major red alert.

"If it wasn't for my obsession with Marta, I might give you a run for your money, kid." Banks grinned when Tosin glared at him.

Sabine laughed. "Aren't you supposed to be the role model around here?"

"Maybe this old dog is learning some of the young dogs' tricks instead." Banks waggled his brows then went back to admiring the last lingering pastel clouds left in the wake of what had been a spectacular sunset.

Tosin would have gone to speak to Kahori, except a woman in a similar—though less extravagant—traditional costume whisked her away. Waverly and Archer made it back and fed him a few scraps of delectable pork and grilled papaya. Just like Kahori's peck this afternoon, the tender meat only made him crave a bigger bite.

Before he could sneak another helping, the drummers assembled in a semi-circle. They stayed within the bamboo poles lying in the sand, which delineated the "stage" for tonight's performances.

People crowded together as they settled down and gave their full attention to the collection of men who began to play as one. The primal thundering of their fists and tapered sticks on hollowed out logs and sharkskin drumheads mesmerized Tosin along with the rest of the audience.

As the last of the sunlight faded, dozens of tiki torches were lit. Flames flickered, casting dancing shadows onto the beach. The soft slap of gentle waves accompanied the music made by dozens of hands acting in unison. If he closed his eyes, Tosin could imagine this place and similar humans entertaining themselves the same way a thousand years ago.

Even still, in all the time in between then and now, he was sure a woman as captivating as Kahori had never existed. She confirmed his theory when the drummers parted and admitted her into their midst. Singing layered on top of the percussion as she began to sway from side to side. She kicked off the show solo, clearly its star. Her arms and hips moved sinuously in an unhurried style that appeared similar to hulas he'd seen in Hawaii, though fiercer and extraordinarily sensual. Tosin overheard one of the local women tell Banks the dance was called the *hura*.

It didn't take long before Tosin had to crumple up a corner of the blanket he sat on to cover his lap, though it might take the entire quilt to camouflage the effect she had on him. Fortunately, he got a bit of a reprieve as the song ended and an ensemble of about a dozen men took her place.

Their power and precision awed him, but it didn't tug at his soul like Kahori had. They performed a fast-paced drum dance, shaking the dried grass tied around their calves furiously with moves that reminded him of exotic birds. Crouched, feet together, they flapped their knees apart then closed triple time to the beat while their arms sliced through the air. Percussive claps and shouts punctuated their actions. Shark-teeth necklaces stood out stark white against their bronzed skin.

They were badass and would definitely have given him pause if he were a rival tribe leader. A group of men so in sync and in shape would be tough to beat on the battlefield.

When he thought he'd seen it all, women began to join them as the men made way. He scanned the troupe for any hint of Kahori.

She wasn't there. Tosin would know in an instant if she was. Still, there was a hell of a lot of bare midriff, soft skin, and undulating abdomens to keep him interested in the change of crew. These women could shake it. Seriously.

As impressive as the guys had been, the women were even more so. Grace tempered the fury of their movements, which were coupled with a walloping helping of seduction.

The instant the music changed, Tosin leaned forward. As he had hoped, Kahori rejoined the dancers. This time two men approached, one from each side of her. Both carried torches. Her features stood out in the harsh lighting, making her appear otherworldly. Strong and worthy of devotion from mere mortals. Sign him the hell up.

As if the image she projected wasn't enough to keep him engrossed, she locked her stare on his before offering him a coy smile.

Tosin gazed into her eyes until something sparked by her side, startling him. It was only then he realized what had happened. The men had lit the contraptions dangling from chains cuffed to her wrists. Now she wielded two actual fireballs.

What the fuck?

Though the sight of her in paraphernalia that reminded him of bondage gear took his fantasies straight to the next level, he wasn't sure it was wise. What if she got burned?

Instead, it was him that began to smolder. If her previous dance had been sensual, this one was a frenzy of passion. The drumming escalated until her hips damn near shook the feathers off the belt that hugged her low around her waist, right where he'd like to lay a trail of open-mouthed kisses.

He hadn't known humans were capable of movement like that.

Twerking had nothing on the *ura rama*.

And all the while, she swung the fireballs in elaborate swirls to the beat. As the song progressed, her tricks got more and more daring. Dangerous.

Tosin's pounding heart threatened to burst as she swung the *poi* behind her back, over her head, and even between her legs. Right where he wanted to be. He imagined fucking to this insane tempo, being driven on by the primordial pulse that matched his crescendoing lust.

Kahori had him lunging half out of his cross-legged position when she appeared to lose her grip on those whirling flames. Instead of crashing into her or the crowd, they landed at her feet in just the right place to ignite a ring of oil he hadn't noticed earlier. She danced on, cocooned in an inferno, dropping into a crouch while still working her hips.

Every man in the place must have imagined what a woman with that kind of muscle memory would be capable of during sex. She could ride him to hell and back, he was sure.

Tosin was ready and willing to let her burn him up all night long.

With one final flourish, the flame extinguished, the drums halted at a dead stop, and the entire beach was plunged into dark silence that rang in his ears. Only the paths of light from Kahori's whirling fireworks, which were probably etched permanently into his eyeballs, remained like the light trail from a sparkler.

Tosin struggled to catch his breath, maybe drawing air into his lungs for the first time in twenty minutes. Beside him Miguel groaned, "Daaaaammmmmnnnnn."

Then applause rang out from everywhere around them. Tosin clapped loudest.

When it died down and the torches around the buffet were lit, the divemasters and their little gang sat speechless despite the line rapidly forming under the food tent.

Sabine gawked at Miguel. "I should smack you for that reaction... But daaaaammmmmmnnnnnnn is right."

Waverly leaned over to ask her, "Do you think Kahori could teach us to do some half-assed version of that?"

Archer and Miguel wore matching grins when Sabine said, "I don't know, but I think we should ask for a lesson."

"I second that motion," Archer said while staring at his girlfriend, as if picturing her in Kahori's place.

Tosin didn't have to make any mental substitutions. He'd never forget what he'd seen tonight. It would be hard to when the woman who'd played the goddess on the stage before him raced around to rejoin them. He tried not to be disappointed when he realized the bottom half of her ornate traditional costume had been swapped for another *pareu*, this time wrapped around her waist and knotted off center at one hip. It was lovely. But he hoped someday he could convince her to give him a private showing of her moves in her full regalia. At least she'd kept the coconut bra.

"That was incredible," Banks said as Archer introduced him.

Waiting for Kahori to thank each of his friends for their lavish praise nearly killed Tosin. But when she worked down the line and finally stood in front of him, he couldn't find the words to tell her how much of an impact her performance had made on him.

"Wow," he breathed as she looked up at him expectantly. "Is there anything you suck at?"

She tipped her head back and laughed, drawing appreciative stares from every man within hearing range. "Plenty of things."

"Yeah, like what?" He couldn't help himself. He reached out and encircled her wrist with his fingers, rubbing the light marks left by her fiery apparatus. If only they were rope marks instead...

"For starters, I wish I'd given you a better kiss earlier." She bit her lip as soon as the confession escaped, as if she hadn't meant to say it aloud.

"I'll give you a do-over." He leaned in, his mouth parting of its own accord.

"Come eat, Kahori," her dad shouted at her. "You must be hungry."

They sprang apart as if busted doing a hell of a lot more than flirting.

After the initial shock wore off, she amazed Tosin by smiling—slow and wide—then holding out her hand to him. "He has no idea how famished I am."

Tosin licked his lips. "Same here."

∽ **SEVEN** ∽

ndorphins released by dancing had clearly made Kahori high.

It was the only reason she could come up with to explain the outrageous remarks she'd made to Tosin. No matter how many times she chastised herself, reminded herself of the dangers, he teased out her inner sex kitten. Hell, she hadn't even known she *had* an inner sex kitten before him.

Stupidly, she kept on indulging the riskiest and most vulnerable aspects of her personality. Yet she couldn't help but want to meet that part of her she'd never before unleashed.

Though Tosin had acted like a perfect gentleman while they ate, praising the cooks as he devoured his meal, all she could see was the way he followed local customs by sucking the rich juices off his fingers one-by-one in compliment and the lingering hunger in his eyes, which food alone couldn't satisfy.

Despite the undercurrents, she found him remarkably easy to talk to. Him *and* his friends. Female companions who were more interested in their careers than immediately raising families were rare in Aitutaki. It was refreshing to have people to talk to who could understand her ambitions.

Knowing that one day, hopefully, Waverly would wear a ring Kahori'd made as a symbol of the woman's partnership with Archer felt rewarding. Kahori had put so much into that piece, it thrilled her to know it had found a worthy home. The evening topped her list of favorite festivals. Memories she'd already made would last long after they'd sailed away again.

For including her in his inner circle, she intended to thank Tosin properly. Plus, make sure she never forgot the way he made her feel simply by being nearby. If his attention alone could make butterflies riot in her belly, what would his passion do?

Melt her completely.

Gathering every scrap of courage she could muster, Kahori drew a deep breath and asked, "Would you like to take a walk? There's a spot not too far from here I'd love to show you."

He stood so fast he drew the attention of several of the village elders, including her father.

Damn!

Banks came to their rescue. "Miguel, Sabine, I think we'd better talk to the council about the algae grow operation before it gets too much later, don't you think? I wouldn't want any of them to leave before they can hear us out, and maybe take a vote."

Genius. Pure, utter, legendary genius.

Tosin murmured, "Thank you."

Before anyone could stop them, Kahori grabbed his hand then half-dragged him toward the lagoon so they could enjoy the view as they walked along its shore. It was easily Aitutaki's best feature. Land only accounted for about six and a half square miles of the atoll. It was comprised of the main mass and fourteen other uninhabited islets—little more than blobs of sand and palms, really—called *motus* around the perimeter. One of those held her uncle's private resort, complete with overwater cabanas and a single spectacular honeymooners' suite. The remaining fifteen or so square miles within the barrier reef consisted of placid, crystal clear water rife with sea creatures.

She didn't have to tug much before Tosin got the idea. They ran over the soft, warm sand with their fingers laced together. By the time they'd reached the placid surface of the trapped sea, a fit of giggles had assaulted them both.

It may not have been a daring escape, but they'd evaded her father's grasp.

Tosin drew her close to his side, his fingers running along the length of one of her necklaces, then murmured, "You know, I've been all over the world. Still, I've never seen a place full of as much beauty as this one."

She might have thought he meant the turquoise water, or the sugary beaches, or the pristine environment, or even the postcard-esque line of palm trees along the deserted stretch of tropical paradise if he hadn't been staring into her eyes.

When he slouched, angling his face toward hers, she shook her head. "Not here."

Sure enough, when she glanced over her shoulder, Hemi and his father, Kimo, monitored her interactions with the *papa'a* from their spots around the council's table.

Tosin nodded, then followed her silently, wandering into the shallows as if he loved the silky feel of the saltwater against his skin as much as she did. Beyond him, on the northwest side of the main island, she could see the impressive boat she knew he'd come from. It was a beautiful one the likes of which they didn't see often around here.

"So you're really a divemaster on that cruise ship?" She'd heard the whispers of the other women backstage tonight, many of them hoping to convince him to guide them on a midnight adventure. During dinner, he'd let Sabine and Waverly talk about themselves and what they did onboard, without insisting on bragging about his own accomplishments. His humble silence had impressed her more than if he'd boasted, but it left her wondering more about him.

"Sort of." Even in the starlight she could see his throat flex as he swallowed. "It's complicated. It didn't used to be. Archer, Miguel, and I traveled all over the world. Diving for a living, visiting new places, and partying with pretty women. That was kind of our thing for a decade."

"It's not anymore?" she wondered.

"Well, you see, Archer sort of inherited six or seven billion dollars. But who's counting?" Tosin laughed, though his humor seemed tinged with disbelief. "He put most of it in a trust for charity stuff. Banks runs—"

"Wait. Banks. Archer. As in Archer Quartermaine. Founder of the Banks Foundation. *That* Banks?" Kahori stopped dead in her tracks. Why hadn't she put it together before now?

Because they seemed so damn normal, and the name on the card he'd given her hadn't been Quartermaine. That's why.

"Uh oh." Tosin grimaced. "I hadn't expected you'd have heard of us. Can we forget I said all that and go back to where we were before?"

"No." She shook her head. "I can't erase my memory like that. But it doesn't really change how I think of you. We are who we are. You're still the guy who brought me flowers. And the guy who nearly crashed into my booth when he first saw me. A divemaster on a really sweet ship. The rest...eh. Not as important."

"Did I mention that I don't just work there? Archer sort of gave Miguel and me each a one-third share in the Divemaster Project, including the boat itself."

"That must make you..."

Tosin nodded. "Rich. I guess. If I ever planned to sell, which I don't. It's everything I've ever dreamed of. A life where I do what I love forever and help make other people happy along the way. I'm the luckiest bastard ever. Doubly so because I'm here, spending this time with you."

Well, that whole "who you are isn't important" thing might not be true after all.

Okay...it was a Big Fat Lie.

Because now she realized clinging to this man for more than tonight would be utterly impossible.

When she didn't reply to that, he tried to lighten the mood some.

Tosin shook his head ruefully, "So you noticed my graceful entrance that day, huh?"

She appreciated the effort. There'd be time to mourn what she could never keep later, when she'd lost it. Right now, she should enjoy.

"I took it as a compliment." She squeezed his hand as she spotted the shadow of her landmark rock up ahead. "Why don't we see if I can show you something that will live up to the incredible sights you must have seen so far on your journey around the world, huh?"

"I'm sure you can, Kahori." He kissed her knuckles then followed her into the crevice between two giant slabs of basalt. It was narrow enough that they had to go single file, at least for a while.

"Are you sure we don't need some sort of lantern?" Tosin asked, sounding unsure after they'd shuffled a couple dozen feet into the cave entrance. "Sharks, eels, sting rays, whatever...underwater stuff never freaks me out. But I'm man enough to admit that if a bat swoops down in my face, you're going to have to give me mouth-to-mouth after I faint."

"Doesn't sound so bad to me." She patted his hand. "Just a little bit farther."

By the time they'd rounded the last bend in the tunnel she knew by heart, a faint light had already began to pulse around them.

"Is that my eyes?" he asked, rubbing his free hand over them.

"Nope. Glowworms."

"Seriously?" Tosin walked a little faster. "I hear water, too. The tide is out right now so that should be okay, right?"

"Yep." It thrilled her that he was so in touch with nature, a quality she could appreciate. "It's safe for a couple more hours. This entire passageway floods at high tide, though."

"Holy shit, wait until I tell Miguel and Archer about this." His enthusiasm energized her further.

But when they passed through the stone archway into the main cavern, his excitement turned to astonishment.

Kahori didn't blame him. It was fairly large, big enough to fit several cottages inside. Stalactites and stalagmites speared throughout like snaggleteeth. Illuminated by the glowworms on the ceiling, they took on hues from navy to teal. On the backside of the cave a waterfall tumbled gently from the ceiling, causing rings that extended out into the otherwise mirror-like surface of the subterranean pool. A stream ran out the other side to rejoin the ocean beyond. Not many living people knew about her secret place—potentially only her and Tosin—but the walls were covered with prehistoric paintings that bonded her to her ancestors, rooting her to a place she hadn't always felt secure in.

Especially after her mother had run off with a tourist when Kahori was a toddler. She supposed she couldn't blame her father for mistrusting Tosin, given the way he'd been betrayed by the love of his life. Kahori was all he had left. Another reason nothing serious could come of her time with Tosin.

Instead, she vowed to enjoy each minute he was there and interested in her to the fullest.

"Is it okay to swim here?" he asked her in a hushed, reverent whisper.

Kahori nodded then began to strip off her clothes. Why hedge? She didn't get the feeling that Tosin would object to nudity. She was about to find out if her impression was correct.

"Fuck yes. You're gorgeous, Kahori." His accent made her name sound special as he ditched his shirt and then his shorts. Bare beneath, he definitely didn't have any qualms about displaying his body to her. Or probably the world.

And why should he? His near-perfect form made her wish she was a sculptor instead of a jeweler. She'd pay particular attention to the distinct lines than ran from his hips to his groin and those that separated his washboard abs. And of course to his impressive cock.

"So are you."

"Show me where it's safe." He held out his hand to her, not afraid to let her lead. She imagined he was used to doing this for his own clients, but he didn't flinch when she navigated the craggy floor.

Kahori took him to the water's edge and beyond. Until her toes no longer touched bottom. She floated on her back, kicking lazily toward the waterfall as she observed the twinkling overhead.

Joining her, Tosin swam alongside her. Quiet for a while, he broke the silence to read her thoughts. "They look like constellations."

"I love looking at the stars," she admitted. "Especially here—they're so bright. When I was traveling to cities, it always made me sad to realize how little those people can see of the world and what's around us. Our people used the stars to find their way across oceans, but there...I was lost."

"Maybe you just needed a better guide." Tosin couldn't possibly know how true that statement was. Thankfully, it seemed like he was about to show her the way.

EIGHT

A few moments later, they reached the far side of the cavern. When it became shallow enough, Tosin stood and tugged Kahori to him. She didn't resist, wrapping her legs around his hips. His hands fit perfectly over her ass, holding her close as he captured her mouth.

He covered her lips with his then, swallowing her soft moan as he kissed her thoroughly enough to curl her toes where they treaded through the water.

Kahori savored her first true kiss, from this man or any other. Her prior interactions hadn't been this affectionate, or as intimate. A sad but true statement on her lack of love life. Instead of dwelling on it, she snatched the opportunity she had now to indulge all the whimsical and romantic fantasies she'd entertained throughout the years.

With the cave sparkling around them and him filling her with equally glittery feelings, she lost herself in their exchange. Making out with him, she lost all sense of time or place. All she knew was the brush of their mouths, and tongues, against each other.

Tosin never let her slip, though eventually he did stride forward until she could perch on one of the stones that had been worn smooth by millennia of erosion.

Before Kahori had grown accustomed to the pure bliss he imparted with his lips and teeth, along with the rub of their torsos against each other, he'd moved on to the curve of her neck. A sharp nip followed by the wet heat of his lick caused her to cry out and cling to his shoulders in an attempt at grounding herself against the onslaught of pleasure.

"Easy," he crooned before wandering lower still to cup her breasts. He weighed and plumped them in his hands, accustoming her to his touch, before taking the tight tip of one into his mouth and flicking his tongue over it. Only when he'd damn near driven her mad with lust did he begin to suck on it, igniting her as easily as the sparks had kindled her *poi* earlier.

Cool water splashed across her skin, helping salve the blistering heat his touch left behind.

And still it shocked her, just how much more pleasurable it was when he kissed a meandering path across her stomach to her mound. The first contact of his mouth on her pussy had her spine arching impossibly. The position only granted him better access to her core.

She spread her legs without bothering to fight him, herself, or the inevitable course of events.

With a groan, he accepted her unspoken invitation. Tosin buried his face in her folds and devoured her slickness. He used his tongue to work her open then inserted one of his long fingers into her body. She clamped down on it, hugging it tight within her.

It felt better than anything she'd ever done to herself, and nothing at all like the pain she'd experienced the last time she'd let a man near her when she was this defenseless.

The bliss Tosin imparted left no room to think about her regrets.

Kahori concentrated on the waves of rapture washing over her along with the stream of the waterfall, which caressed her every place Tosin couldn't reach while otherwise occupied.

It didn't take long before her shouts threatened to crumble the rock walls. Unexpectedly, a strong orgasm hit her. She shuddered and quaked in his arms. His name echoed off the stone and filled the space with proof of her ecstasy.

He chuckled against her body, the amusement sending shockwaves through her sensitized flesh. The softest of tugs on her clit rejuvenated her pleasure, astounding her even as it thrilled her.

Tosin wrecked her. He brought her up and over the peak into climax time and time again until she was utterly boneless and gasping for air. "Mercy."

He lifted his head, smiling as he gathered her in his arms and lowered her into the warm, soothing water so he could place an almost chaste kiss on the corner of her gaping mouth. "Sorry, I got a little carried away. You taste so fucking sweet, and sound even better. It felt amazing when you came on my hand, too. I could never get enough of that. But I'd like to try."

His frank speech set off aftershocks that rattled her to her bones. What was she doing? She was so out of her league with him. Too late, she realized that she might have swum too far out to sea to make it back to shore.

A rookie mistake. One she might not survive.

This had been foolish. And she would pay the price.

Because now that she knew what she was missing, she would never be happy with life the way it had been. Not ever again. She'd destroyed her own haven as surely as the strongest typhoon slamming into the island could have.

The best she could hope for was to make it worth it.

It would help to know she hadn't only taken from him, but had given a part of herself as well.

"Will you show me how to please you?" she asked.

"Pretty much the same way as you do it with any other guy. Mouth on cock. Can't go wrong with that recipe." Tosin chuckled as he released her. He planted one hand behind him on the rock she'd so recently occupied then leapt so that he ended up seated there at the perfect height for her attentions. Water sluiced off of him in rivulets that drew her eyes steadily downward. To his—*wow*.

She floated closer until she could wrap one arm around his waist. Her other hand reached for his thick shaft, hovering a fraction of an inch away. Her fingers shook with her desire to do this well.

"Show me?" she repeated, hoping he wouldn't sense how artless she truly was.

No such luck. "Kahori..."

She refused to meet his probing stare, instead studying his erection close up.

"Look at me." He cupped her chin and pressed upward with gentle yet steady pressure until she did as he asked. "You're not a virgin, are you?"

"Not exactly," she hedged.

"It's really a yes or no sort of thing, isn't it?" His eyes were wider now, his pupils darker and growing. Did her lack of experience make him angry? Or was he getting even more turned on by the prospect of her near innocence? "Tell me what you mean before we go any further."

When she didn't answer right away, he softened the harsh rasp of his voice. His placid veneer in no way diminished his authority. It reassured her that he had everything under control. That he wouldn't rush her or take for the sake of taking.

Unlike before…

"I don't want to hurt you, Kahori. Or frighten you. Tell me what I need to know to take care of you properly. That's all I care about." He brushed the pad of his thumb across her lower lip.

Without thinking, she opened her mouth and took it inside for a moment. The entire time she toyed with it she imagined what it would feel like to do something similar with his cock, which was much, *much* bigger than the digit she rolled her tongue across.

"Don't distract me," he grumbled as he withdrew. "Talk to me."

She gave him the general idea. "There's no one on the island I'm interested in building a life with. No one I could have something casual with either. That's not how things work here. An affair would become political. Families would be involved. Before I'd even figured out if I could stand to share a house with a man, we'd be married. Just…no. There's no opportunity for fun without strings. So when I went on one of my trips, I did some research and found a club."

"What kind of club, sweetheart?" Tosin seemed still and calm, but she could sense a storm brewing within him.

"A sex club. It didn't mean anything, and it wasn't what I'd had in mind. I—" She shook her head. "I did it, but it didn't count for much besides going through the motions. I don't want to talk about it now. Don't want to ruin tonight with the ghosts of my poor decisions. So, please. I need some help making sure I'm doing this right, okay?"

His nostrils flared and his cheeks flushed in response to her entreaty. She'd definitely struck some kind of chord with him. She only wished she knew what it was. "I'll give you anything you need tonight, I swear. Come here."

He reached down and grabbed her beneath her arms, hoisting her up until he could crush his mouth over hers. The kiss he gave her then was ten times as potent as the ones before. His desperation transmitted something deeper, more genuine. It matched hers.

Ultimately he lowered her with a sigh, then reclined on one straight-locked arm that he braced behind him on the rock. "Start by running your fingers along my dick and balls. Lightly. Explore. See how they feel in your hands. Then against your tongue."

When his words alone threatened to shake her apart again, she stared up at him.

"Go ahead." He took her hand in his then placed it around his shaft and stroked himself some using her fingers for his gratification. Encouragement, yes. Force, no.

He let go, allowing her to proceed at her own pace, so very different from the last time she'd been this bold.

Kahori wondered at the blend of steel and softness against her hand. Even more so, she admired his restraint. Not once did he rush her as she took her time learning every inch of him and how her caresses affected him.

Each time he groaned, or cursed, or hissed, her smile widened. By the time a pearly drop of precome beaded on the very tip of his hard-on, she felt rather pleased with herself.

Tosin clearly agreed. He sank his fingers into her hair and nudged her nearer. "If you want to, you can taste me."

If she could have purred, she might have when she considered the possibility of returning the pleasure he'd gifted to her with his talented mouth. She parted her lips then surged upward until his cock was level with her face.

Kahori reached her tongue out, tentatively at first, and flicked it against him. She swiped the fluid from him and tested it out. Not bad. Even better was the hitch in his breathing, which grew heavier by the second. She could do that to him.

It revealed a power she hadn't known she possessed.

The feeling reminded her of the rush she experienced when dancing, except multiplied a thousand times. She was the focus of his rapt attention. The means to his ecstasy.

Tired of tiptoeing around, she opened her mouth wide and attempted to swallow him whole, like she'd seen women in porn do to their partners. Unfortunately, she choked.

"Not so fast. You don't have to do that to make it feel incredible." He lifted her and held her steady, keeping her from floundering while she recovered. "The most sensitive part is here."

Tosin took his cock in his fist and tapped the underside against her lips. She stuck out her tongue and swiped it just below the ridge of the head. He gasped.

So she did it again and again.

And when he let her have more of him, she settled for suckling on just the fat tip of his hardening cock, surprised when she realized he hadn't even been fully erect earlier. Damn.

Kahori took her time, testing different places and alternating sucking, licking, and massaging. She found that when she bobbed over his cockhead while swirling her tongue along the underside of his shaft, he began to tense.

The addition of her hand cupping his balls, rolling them as she marveled at the unique texture of his skin there, seemed to ramp up his pleasure. When she found something he liked, she did it more, harder and faster until her fun drove him to the edge of his self-control.

"I'm close, Kahori." She didn't consider the fact that he was also warning her that she was about to have a mouthful of his come until he froze, then bucked beneath her.

Tosin growled, making her wish she had a hand free to rub her clit while he pumped his release down her throat. It turned her on to witness his surrender to rapture. She drank him down, relieved to have pleased him, thrilled to have enjoyed it herself, honored to have some sliver of him to carry with her when they went their separate ways.

Kahori still sucked softly when he nudged her shoulders, urging her back.

As she withdrew, he slipped from between her lips. Except...

"Did I do it right?" she asked, peeking up at him from beneath her lashes.

"Hell yeah." He could hardly catch his breath enough to pant those two words she needed to believe so desperately. But—

"Then why are you still hard?" she wondered, embarrassed by her ignorance. "Is that...uh...normal?"

Tosin cracked up. "I have a feeling that with you it would be. Yeah."

"So you want me to do it again? Over and over, like you did to me?" Kahori licked her lips. She'd loved having him in her mouth and wouldn't mind practicing her newfound techniques to drive him wild. It was fun. Exhilarating. Empowering.

"I have a better idea." He slid into the water beside her then wrapped her in a tight hug before kissing her forehead lightly. The length of his shaft nudged her pussy.

If she angled her hips...

"Whoa. Hang on a second." Tosin cursed.

"Hmm? Why?"

"Condoms. They're in the pocket of my shorts." He shoved off the boulder and swam for the opposite side of the pool as if he were attempting to qualify for the Olympics, or being stalked by a shark. The drag caused by his substantial erection didn't seem to slow him down either.

Kahori grinned as she gave chase. She couldn't wait to sink her teeth into him.

His fine ass, which reflected the glowworms dotting the ceiling, seemed like a good enough place to start. By the time she had reached the edge of the water, he was returning with a foil packet in hand. He ripped it open then sheathed himself quickly and efficiently. Virginal he was not.

Kahori had a moment of doubt.

What did this mean to him? To her? Was she doing the right thing this time?

It was nearly impossible to think when every instinct screamed for her to fuck him while she could. That ferocious side of herself frightened her a little.

So when he sank over her in the shallows and began to lavish praise and charm on her in between tender kisses, a seed of guilt began to grow. Her passion began to fade and logic crept into the void it left behind.

"I'm glad we have tonight," she said as she tried to reassure herself that it was okay to savor what she could even if it was only a drop in the ocean of what she wanted.

"One night like this could never be enough," Tosin whispered. "I'm going to want a hell of a lot more of your sweetness. Don't you realize this is only the beginning? Ah, Kahori. Maybe I'll take you with me."

He groaned at the painful reminder that their time was limited. Or might even have already run out.

Just like that, she felt as if her blazing *poi* had smashed into her, scorched her, and raised painful blisters over her entire body. Especially in the vicinity of her heart.

What was she doing? She could never abandon her homeland or her *pāpā* like her mother had. It would kill him.

Despite her desires, she could never be so selfish.

Tosin made her spirit soar even as he shattered her illusions. Because she didn't have anything else to give this moment. Nothing more could come of their illicit interlude. And if she was teasing him by indulging their desires temporarily when she had no intention of pursuing their attraction after the first light of dawn, then she was only using him as others had done to her.

That kind of behavior she would not tolerate from herself.

"I—I can't." She shoved his shoulders, rolling him off of her, then staggered to her feet, leaving him crashed on the ground with empty arms and a monster erection. Add mortification to her agony. "I have to go. I'm sorry. I've made a mistake. A big one. I can't do this. I'm leaving before I make it worse."

"Kahori, wait. I'm an idiot for assuming you wanted more, too. I wasn't thinking. I'll take anything you want to give me and be grateful for it. I didn't mean that like it sounded." He grimaced when she kept backing away toward her clothes. "Hang on. If you're going, at least let me walk you home."

"That's not a good idea." She shook her head. Her father would take one look at them and know what she had done. How she'd betrayed him. Not only by fooling around with an outsider, but by considering what it might be like to leave this place behind. To be greedy enough to want to spend endless nights in Tosin's bed, damn the consequences.

Maybe she was her mother's daughter after all.

Kahori flung her *pareu* around her, cinching it closed with a well-practiced twist.

Though Tosin attempted to catch her, he didn't know the path as well as her and the darkness between the glowworm cavern and the sea meant he had to inch his way forward while his vision adjusted.

When she heard him cursing violently behind her, she winced. Sounded like he'd stubbed a toe. Hopefully he hadn't broken his whole damn foot.

Add another black mark to her tally. She'd repaid him poorly for the pleasure he'd given her.

Staying would only make it worse for them both.

Once on the beach, Kahori cut inland. Tosin would never be able to track her through the thick jungle on the shortcut she sometimes took to her house.

Unfortunately, the other men who'd been lying in wait—searching for her around the rocks where their sandy footprints had vanished—would have no similar troubles.

❧ NINE ❧

Kahori ran. The underbrush became thin green switches that whipped her cheeks, her arms, and the uncovered upper swells of her breasts. She didn't feel the sting. At least not until her tears dripped salt into the open wounds.

How could a night that had held so much potential turn into another mess?

Was she making everything worse?

She slowed from her dash to a jog and finally to a stagger, until the uncertainty and pain overcame her. Bracing her palms on her knees, she bent in half, trying to catch her breath and think clearly. Should she go back to Tosin? Beg him to forgive her waffling and confusion? At least explain what had set her off?

For a normally levelheaded person, being frightened and erratic—out of control in the face of her conflicted emotions—didn't sit well with her. Her cowardice disgusted her. Drawing herself up tall, Kahori glanced over her shoulder toward the beach.

Tosin bellowed her name. If he wasn't careful he'd draw attention from the island night guests, which was the very last thing she needed. Every nosy neighbor and town gossip would hear of their tiff, then speculate about what had caused it. Shit, had he even bothered to pull on his shorts before charging after her?

If not, she'd have a lot of explaining to do.

She had to turn around, if only to calm him so that he didn't shout the whole place to the ground or tear the jungle apart searching for her. She got the feeling he wasn't the type of man to give up easily.

Kahori took a single step in that direction before jumbled movement in the leaves surrounding her caught her attention. It wasn't breezy. The disturbance grew too big to have been caused by a bird or even a wild boar. Someone was out there.

"Tosin?" she called softly even as the hairs on her nape stood up.

Her luck had run out this evening. It wasn't her almost-lover. Instead, four men wearing black hoods and dark clothing emerged from the dense foliage. They stalked nearer, closing in around her like a casting net about to scoop up a school of fish.

"Who are you?" She stumbled backward, tripping over a vine before righting herself. Something told her that if she fell now, she wouldn't be getting back up.

"You know, don't you, Kahori?"

Hell, no. She didn't and she didn't want to either. So she attempted to flee through one of the gaps before it was too late.

For one glorious moment, she thought she'd slipped out of their grasp. Until her hair pulled taut and wrenched her backward. One of them must have grabbed a fistful as she darted past.

Kahori's instinctive scream pierced the night. "Help!"

This time it was terror, not pleasure, that echoed across the island.

Sleeping animals roused and charged deeper into the cover of darkness. She wished she could fly away as easily from the crushing impact of someone tackling her. The crack of her temple striking a log or a rock or something at least as dense as her skull ricocheted through her head. Her vision doubled before slowing refocusing.

"Where is he?" the man on top of her, pinning her to the dirt, snarled. His hot, stinky breath and aggression reminded her of the things she'd been trying to forget this evening.

"Get the fuck off me!" She lashed out—kicking, scratching, attempting to bite. Anything possible to inflict pain before he could.

Too late.

The man backhanded her, driving her teeth into her lips. An iron tang burst across her taste buds.

"You bastard! HELP!" she screamed again, projecting as loudly as she could manage.

This time she prayed Pāpā, Hemi, Uncle Kimo— or anyone else for that matter—could hear her after all. Let the entire village come running. She no longer gave a shit who saw. They had zero tolerance for violence. This would not go unpunished.

Hopefully she would be alive to see justice served.

"Now you've done it. We don't have much time. Someone's going to hear you squawking. So tell me...where is he? And where's the good stuff? You can't fool us with our own tricks, *yariman*."

"Who? Tosin? What?" That rock must have rattled her brains. Nothing her attacker said made sense.

"Play dumb if you like. We'll get what we're owed however we can. Let this be a lesson about what happens when you cheat us." One of the other guys kicked her in the ribs, knocking the wind out of her. She couldn't have asked more questions or raised a ruckus if she'd wanted to. "Tell him next time we won't stop here. Next time we'll take you and sell you to anyone willing to pay for your pussy until you work off his debt."

If that threat was supposed to subdue Kahori, they had miscalculated.

Instead, she redoubled her efforts to get loose. They might not have been very effective at warding off his blows, but at least they may have slowed the pummeling of his fists or impaired his aim.

Who would do this to her? Why?

Because she'd shown interest in Tosin? Because they wanted what she'd nearly given him?

Pure insanity. The sexy divemaster didn't deserve the wrath of small-minded losers, who apparently hated him on sight. Or because he'd taken something they considered *theirs*. Kahori had known there were still some extremely strong traditions on her island home. But this... She never would have expected this.

Another instant her faith in her fellow humans shattered.

This time cut deeper.

Her own people had turned on her. Or had they? Why didn't she recognize the voice of her attacker? Surely she knew everyone on Aitutaki.

It was impossible to think when they took turns waling on her now.

Kahori screeched and tried to crawl away, which only presented the perfect opening for them to drag her back by her hair again. As she lurched to the side, she felt the fine strings of her coconut bra snap. Someone grabbed her bared breast with bruising force.

Her thrashing weakened as horror bogged down her reaction time.

Hyperventilation didn't help either. Lightheadedness mixed with agony and despair.

She cowered on the ground, flinching from the fist that flew toward her face.

TEN

Tosin had barely stumbled out of the cave and onto the beach, his foot throbbing worse than it had that time a sea urchin had used it as a pin cushion, when he heard Kahori scream.

It wasn't a sound of anger or frustration.

No, it was fear.

Terror with pain mixed in.

Fuck! Had she fallen? Hurt herself in the darkness worse than he had? "Kahori!"

The following silence nearly frightened him more. Then another cry rang out, this one more urgent. It came from within the jungle. How the hell would he find her in there?

Glancing down, he tapped the face of his watch, a dive model complete with compass. He was an expert at navigating with it. Sometimes the divemasters tested themselves. One of them would keep his eyes closed as his partners hauled him to a random spot on the reef to see if he could find his way home. Tosin had never lost that little game yet.

Tosin took off after her.

He might not know where he was headed, but he could damn sure make it out again once he'd reclaimed Kahori. There was no doubt in his mind that he would. He wasn't letting her go that easily. And he sure as shit wasn't going to let her suffer out there, alone, because the thought of burying himself in her pretty pussy over and over had caused him to lose his motherfucking mind and say stupid stuff.

Tosin had spooked her bad.

Ironically enough, he seemed to have done the damage with words most of his other playmates would have killed to hear him speak. He tried to think about how he would fix things when he found her to distract from the anxiety her escalating shouts caused in him.

He needed to stay steady, keeping track of his landmarks and compass readings, in order to find her then bring her out again safely. Losing his calm and charging toward her might get him there faster, but then they'd be stuck. And it sounded like she might need immediate medical attention.

Tosin wiped sweat off his brow as he grew closer. Except maybe someone had beat him to her? He could swear he heard the rumbling of a masculine voice up ahead.

"You bastard! HELP!" Kahori begged.

Then nothing could stop him. It hadn't been a simple tumble that had downed her. Someone was mauling her! A person? Who the hell was out here hunting her?

Tosin took one final reading off his compass then crashed through every bit of foliage in the direct path between it and the struggle he could now hear clearly. A worthless motherfucker threatened her, spouting a bunch of nonsense, and then more rustling and grunts followed.

Was that Kahori fighting so viciously?

Pride and panic swirled together as he burst into the tiny clearing where she was being abused then launched himself at her assailant.

"Kahori!" Tosin roared her name like a war cry as he flew across the open area and intercepted one hell of a punch. It didn't do much more than inconvenience him as it drove into his side, but it could have smashed the delicate bones in her cheeks or caused irreparable damage to her more delicate parts, like her eyes or her brain.

Fury the likes of which he'd never experienced before surged within him. He kicked the fucker directly in the chest, throbbing foot be damned. The impact knocked the asshole back at least ten feet from Kahori, onto his ass. He must not have been as stupid as he was evil because he took one look at Tosin's unholy fury and took off, scrambling into the dense foliage. His cronies followed right behind.

Tosin looked between their retreating forms and Kahori, who sprawled in the dirt. She spit out a mouthful of blood then covered her bared breasts with one arm before attempting to stand.

"Catch them," she ordered.

He might have tried if she hadn't collapsed to the ground again, disoriented and wounded.

With a final lingering glare in the direction the men had disappeared, Tosin cursed viciously. He ignored her command. Instead, he rushed to her side and gathered her into his arms. "Fuck them. I'm not leaving you."

He didn't waste time with stupid questions like "Are you okay?" when she clearly was *not* okay.

Tosin cradled her as carefully as he could, somewhat alarmed that she didn't object and instead burrowed her face into the crook of his neck while she trembled in his grip. He glanced at the compass on his wrist then began to work backward.

He still had a ways to go when familiar voices called to him. Archer yelled, "Tosin!"

"Over here," he shouted in return, still angling for the shore.

"What the fuck, man?" Miguel asked when they practically collided with him.

Apparently he hadn't been the only one who'd heard Kahori's screams.

"I've got her. Someone jumped her. They ran away, heading northeast." He turned down the volume when Archer, Miguel, and Banks came into view. "Where's Waverly?"

"Standing by at the chopper with Sabine," Archer replied. She'd spent the afternoon giving kids rides and admiring the aerial view. They'd never expected they'd need her services for an evacuation tonight. "She'll be ready to take off the moment you get there."

Banks crooned to Kahori while the guys made their plans. He inspected her for obvious injuries as he tried to calm her. "Poor girl, look what they did to you. Tosin's going to get you fixed up, okay?"

She nodded then clung to him tighter, as if the twitch of movement was enough to cause her more suffering. They had to get the fuck out of here.

"Will you guys find her father for me? Let him know what's happening. See if anyone can figure out where those guys went and who they are, why they did this to her. I'm not waiting around in case they come back. I'm taking Kahori to the doctor on the *Divemaster*. Then I'm locking her in my cabin where she'll be safe." Tosin had already started walking.

Though he trod carefully, each step jarred Kahori enough to elicit groans from between her split lips. She stirred, seeming like she might object, so he added, "Convince him to come to the ship with you guys. She's going to need him by her side."

"Thank you," Kahori managed to croak. It seemed to sap the last of her energy. The next time her eyelids drooped, they didn't reopen.

So he gave up trying to be gentle and sprinted for the makeshift helipad.

~ ELEVEN ~

Kahori gasped as she came to. Something tickled her nose and the back of her throat. She coughed and flailed as her brain stem flashed warning signals throughout her body.

"Calm down. There's no need to be frightened." A warm female voice soothed some of her panic. "Those were smelling salts. Strong stuff, I know."

Kahori blinked, trying to focus on the people surrounding her in a well-lit room that smelled slightly of lemony disinfectant. She attempted to sit up. A hand rested on her shoulder, keeping her in place. Though she wanted to swat it away, her arms felt heavy and sluggish.

"It's just me," Tosin said. "I'm not trapping you here. I just don't want you to fall off this gurney and injure yourself more."

"Where am I?" She tried to remember what had happened after she left him in the glowworm cavern. Had she hit her head on an outcropping of rock as she fled like an idiot from the pleasure he'd tried to give her?

It certainly throbbed like a bitch.

"I brought you to the *Divemaster* so Dr. Kleveno could evaluate you." He ran his fingers lightly through her hair, thankfully avoiding the side that ached. "It doesn't look like anything's broken. Some of those bruises and scrapes are pretty nasty, though."

Bruises and scrapes? "What happened?"

"You don't remember?" the doctor asked, sounding slightly more concerned. "You might have a mild concussion."

As the woman prodded and poked Kahori, testing her reflexes and the dilation of her pupils with a penlight that stabbed her eyeballs as if it were an ice pick, bits and pieces began to return to her. By the time she remembered everything, her fists had bunched and she shoved past Tosin's restraint to sit upright.

"Those bastards!" She turned to Tosin, regretting the jerk of her head when the room wobbled a bit. "Please tell me you caught them."

He grimaced then shook his head. Negative. "Archer, Miguel, and Banks stayed behind to give it a go and fill in your dad. They're going to bring him here when they're finished with the hunt."

The fact that they weren't back already meant they probably hadn't been any more successful in rounding up her attackers than Tosin had. Damn!

Mostly she wanted to understand *why* they'd done it.

A light knock sounded at the door. Tosin plucked her *pareu* from a plastic chair next to the hospital bed and flapped it to fling off most of the dirt and sticks. The blood would never come out. Besides, it had ripped in a couple spots. It had been her favorite. Ah well. Could be worse.

Kahori lifted her arms so he could wrap it loosely around her like a giant bath towel. It would do for the moment.

Then Tosin went to the door and opened it a crack. Even here he didn't seem to be taking any chances with her security. Despite the evening's trauma, she felt protected and sheltered. Immune to the fear that would probably grip her while dreaming for a while.

"It's our captain," Tosin said over his shoulder.

"Let him in." Kahori shrugged. It seemed silly to make them talk through a gap in the door when she was decent and he might have information she'd like to hear firsthand.

"You're sure?" Tosin asked. She nodded.

When he admitted the man, who was probably around Banks' age, she smiled. Or at least she tried to. When her lips stung, she thought she might have reopened one of the cuts there. Dr. Kleveno was quick to daub some petroleum jelly on the area to keep it pliable. Kahori lifted her finger to the tender site, shocked by how puffy it was. Hey, maybe it gave her a sexy pout, she thought, trying to make the most of an awful situation. It was that or break down, and she didn't want to go that route. It would only make her pounding headache worse.

The new arrival studied her intently as he approached. "Captain Alex," he said in an efficient, staccato greeting that seemed as no-nonsense as the man himself. Fine silver lines in his otherwise dark hair and well-trimmed beard granted him an air of authority appropriate for the person ultimately responsible for the entire *Divemaster*. He was a little taller than average and sturdily built. He wouldn't be easy to push over in any sense of the phrase.

Kahori knew men like Archer, Miguel, Tosin, and Banks wouldn't entrust the ship and their own lives to just anyone. Dr. Kleveno stared at the captain as if he were a legend in his own right. Though she was easily ten—or even fifteen—years younger than the captain, Dr. Kleveno seemed awfully interested in him. She pushed her purple glasses up her freckled nose with her index finger. Possibly so she could see him better.

Trying not to grin, Kahori peeked at Tosin. He was glancing between the two crew members with interest. Meddling matchmakers on Aitutaki would have hooked those two up in a second.

When the captain held out his hand to Kahori, she shook it. He held her in a surprisingly gentle grip. She figured her torn nails and bruised knuckles had something to do with his overabundance of caution. Either that or she looked like the kind of woman who required a delicate touch.

Compared to Waverly, Sabine, and Dr. Kleveno, Kahori wasn't sure she stacked up to the strong females he was used to, though she planned to change his mind. "Nice to meet you, though I wish it were under different circumstances."

"I have a feeling we would have been introduced to each other soon enough no matter what." He looked pointedly at Tosin, who had parked himself at her side like a guard dog. Then Captain Alex asked, "If it's not too upsetting, can you tell me anything you remember that might help identify the people who hurt you? Either of you, really. The guys radioed in. They could use direction."

"When I ran up, I heard one of the guys threatening her. They were interrogating her." Tosin punched his fist into his opposite palm. "I couldn't quite hear it all. More of their tone than the specifics, really."

Her memory was still sort of foggy, but his nugget of information jogged her recollection. "They kept asking me where *he* was. Where the *good stuff* was, too. They also called me some kind of insult when I couldn't figure out who or what they meant. It sounded like *yariman*, which isn't a Māori word or one in any of the Cook Islands dialects that I know."

Captain Alex tensed, his face turning purple. He didn't look at her when he explained, "It's Japanese for slut." When Tosin shot him a bewildered look, the guy shrugged. "I was stationed in Okinawa for nearly four years during my time in the Navy."

Kahori shuddered. "I guess that makes sense. Tosin's right. They did threaten me. They said something about getting what they were owed, even if it meant...uh...selling me."

There really wasn't a more polite way to say that they'd planned to whore her out to rapists, was there?

Tosin growled. He breathed hard, reacting more strongly than she would have imagined to that bit of news.

"I'm sure they were only bluffing." She patted his forearm. "Trying to scare me."

Which had worked, by the way. Though she didn't intend to highlight her cowardice for them.

"Have you had dealings with any Japanese buyers lately?" Captain Alex asked her.

"Thanks to modern technology, I do ship all over the world. We send out orders once a week. I don't remember there being any to Japan in the past month or so, though. Nothing major for certain." She shrugged halfheartedly. "It has to be some sort of mix-up."

"That's a hell of a swing and a miss if so." Tosin wrapped his arm around her and scooted her closed to his side. "Regardless, no one's getting near you again. I swear it."

Kahori leaned against Tosin, closing her eyes. All she really wanted was to lie down somewhere dark and comfortable until her *pāpā* arrived, hopefully with some explanations.

"Can I take her to my cabin now? Is it okay for her to sleep?" Tosin asked Dr. Kleveno, who nodded.

She spoke directly to Kahori when she said, "Unless you'd prefer to stay in here. We have rooms set up for the people en route to participate in Sabine's trials."

"Thank you." She appreciated the out ,though it wasn't necessary. "I'd rather go with him."

"I don't blame you." Dr. Kleveno grinned. "I would too if I were you. The offer stands if you change your mind. There's room and I can keep an eye on you. Otherwise, I'll come check on you in a few hours and bring your next dose of painkillers."

Then she turned to Tosin. "Don't let her get out of bed unless it's to use the bathroom."

"I can do that." He nodded, taking his caretaker duties very seriously.

When Kahori would have hopped down, Tosin scooped her into his arms instead. Captain Alex opened the door so they could pass. "I hope you're feeling better soon. It pains me to admit it, at the risk of overinflating their egos, but these kids have excellent taste in women. You're going to fit right in here."

Kahori winced. She wouldn't be onboard long enough to become integrated into their gang. Why did that thought upset her? The captain's compliments meant a lot in any case. "Thank you."

She tried to stay alert as Tosin carried her through the ship. It was gorgeous. Beyond anything she could have imagined even after the luxurious hotel stays she'd splurged on every once in a while for her business trips.

"I can't believe that Archer—all of you—have pockets deep enough to own all this, and yet he chose to buy Waverly a ring from my shop. Now I get why he asked you about whether he was doing the right thing by not opting for a more traditional stone." She sighed. "He could always give her my ring for her birthday or Christmas or something and pick up a mega-diamond worthy of a billionaire's wife."

"Believe it or not, he's not like that. Waverly isn't either." Tosin laughed. "None of us are. I hope it doesn't disappoint you that I might technically be rich, but I'm still a poor slob at heart. That ring is perfect for her. You'll see when he gives it to her."

Kahori winced. "Yeah. You'll have to videotape his proposal if you can. I'd love to see it." Because surely they'd be long gone before he popped the question.

In fact, after today, maybe they'd be departing sooner than scheduled. She wouldn't blame them for leaving this mess in their rearview mirror. If megayachts even had rearview mirrors.

Staying silent, the craftsman in her settled for observing the fine woodwork and blown glass waves that enhanced the interior of the space as they made their way to the other side of the ship where the owners' quarters were. Right about the time she suspected Tosin had walked halfway back to Aitutaki, he stopped in front of his door and keyed in a code.

Unlike Dr. Kleveno, he didn't ask her where she wanted to sleep. Which was fine by her.

If she was being honest, she couldn't stomach the thought of being alone when she drifted off. Didn't care to wake up by herself in an unfamiliar place, either.

He set her on her feet long enough to slip the *pareu* from around her and toss it into a wad in the corner of his enormous quarters. She didn't blame him. It horrified her that she might stain something in his gleaming, pristine personal space. The linens on the enormous bed were the same steel blue as his eyes. Drawings of fish and sea creatures hung in shiny metal frames, and the modern shelving around the desk held an assortment of orchids and nanogardens.

It immediately felt like a place she could be comfortable.

Ridiculously so.

Though he kept the blackout curtains closed for now—*thank you*—she'd bet there was a spectacular view out the wall-to-wall windows opposite the bed. Tosin peeled back the thick comforter and helped her settle creakily in the plush nest. Though not in too much pain, she felt like a hundred year old elder.

It didn't surprise her when he tugged his shirt over his head, then tucked his thumbs in his waistband and shoved his shorts down with a single slick movement. In the dim light, she couldn't see as much of his spectacular body as she wished she could.

Tosin took his fancy watch off and placed it neatly on the nightstand. She was surprised to see the bracelet he'd bought from her shop lying next to it.

He picked it up and ran his fingers across the intricate carvings she'd slaved over for an inordinate period of time considering the set wasn't a big-ticket item. Then he sat on the edge of the mattress and held it out to her, along with his wrist. "Can you put it on me?"

She flexed her fingers a few times and found them less stiff than they'd been before. Dr. Kleveno must have slipped her some anti-inflammatories. "Sure."

It took her a couple of tries but she managed to fit the black pearl knotted on the end through the leather loop that held it closed. He smiled as he looked at her work adorning him. "I like having this reminder of you on me. I'm not planning on taking this off any time soon."

If Kahori had been a bolder woman, she might have asked for him to put the matching one on her. But she was afraid he might misinterpret that as some kind of commitment, when really she was thinking about a memento of their liaison that she could take out and sigh over after he'd left her behind.

"Mind if I snuggle with you while you rest?" He grinned. "Don't tell the guys, but it's right at the top of my list of favorite bedroom activities."

Kahori snorted then patted the bed beside her. "Yeah, right."

He laughed, but he did seem content as he cradled her against his chest. The lulling thump of his heartbeat helped her settle down. At least until she looked at where her fingers rested on his rib and realized he hadn't escaped their earlier fiasco unscathed. A huge bruise marked the spot that had intercepted that final punch.

If he hadn't shown up right then…

Kahori leaned over and placed a light kiss over the damaged area. "I'm sorry."

"That is in no way your fault." His tone turned icy. "I won't let you blame yourself for something some fuckface did."

"I shouldn't have run from you. Will you let me explain?" She couldn't believe she was offering this part of her—so personal, something that shamed her. But he deserved to understand. It was all she could offer despite everything she wished she could give him.

"Don't feel you have to. But I *am* curious." He rubbed her shoulders lightly, relaxing her further.

His unconditional acceptance made it easier to begin her confession.

⌒ TWELVE ⌒

Tosin concentrated on lying still and keeping his respiration measured. He didn't want to frighten Kahori away again, especially not when she was putting so much faith in him. Trust was something he sensed didn't come easily for her, for some reason he hoped he was about to discover.

If they were going to play again, harder next time, he had to be sure she would enjoy the same brand of loving he did. He couldn't deny his dominant streak, though he could definitely tailor how it manifested to suit her needs. The way she'd deferred to him, begging for instruction in the glowworm cavern, made him positive she could enjoy his hardwired sexual preferences as much as he did. Even if she didn't understand the various nuances of what a power exchange could entail...yet.

It didn't have to be something artificial with a lot of rules of engagement or anything too extreme. He'd love to educate her about the wide variety of pleasures available for her to sample.

Their easy companionship convinced him they would be great partners in and out of bed. But he had to find an approach to intimacy that would work for them both. Challenge accepted.

To do that, he had to understand her first. Her fears, her hopes, her triggers, her limits—each critical variable in the equation. So he kept quiet and studied her, greedily absorbing every crumb of information she fed him about the woman he was quickly becoming obsessed with.

Okay, fine, he'd been completely infatuated with Kahori since the first moment he'd laid eyes on her.

"I guess it started when my mom left us." She drew a deep, shaky breath, wincing slightly when the inhalation put pressure on her ribs. "I was still a toddler. I hardly remember her, to be honest. But I clearly recall how miserable Pāpā was after she had gone. He's always loved Aitutaki. Not only the place, but also the way of living. Truly enjoying each day instead of slaving away in an office, paid to perform a meaningless, repetitive task. He spends time on the water fishing for dinner, on walks through the jungle picking fruit. He soaks up the sun as he repairs our house. Pāpā is resourceful, making things we need out of what we have. So I guess when my mother left, it wasn't only that she abandoned us both and piled a heap of extra responsibilities on him, but she rejected his dying way of life, jabbing another knife in its back."

Tosin could see how that would hurt. What if he'd fallen for a woman who loved living in one place, maybe in a giant city far from the ocean? How could he choose between the person he loved and the only existence that could keep him happy?

He thought about it some more, wondering what might have happened if his grandparents had lived longer. Of course he would have relished every moment he got to spend with them. One day, though, would he have resented being held captive in a place he'd been born in but didn't love as much as others?

As shitty of a grandson as it made him, the answer was probably yes. Then again, they had always encouraged him to follow his heart. They wouldn't have guilted him into staying or anything like that. Still... he thought he understood where she was heading with this.

"So when your business started taking off, you hung around, sacrificing some potential to keep from trampling your dad's heart all over again, right?" Tosin could see how it would be a tough call. There wasn't any clear right answer.

"Yeah." Kahori sighed as if she'd never admitted it out loud before. "I would love to see more of the world than our little island, even though I do think this is probably as close to paradise as I could ever find. But I've felt like I had to tamp down those desires so that I didn't turn out like my mother. Every time I went on one of my selling trips, Pāpā would hug me so tight at the airport that I'm sure he thought I wouldn't come back. Twenty years after my mother split, he's still traumatized. As far as I know, he's never been with anyone else before or since. Who could walk away from their child and husband—one who loved her to his core—like that?"

"Hey, no judgment here." He cleared his throat, then said, "My mom's a hooker."

Kahori giggled. "Come on, I was being serious."

"So was I." He let that truth-bomb explode all over them.

"Wow." She hugged him. "I'm sorry. I shouldn't have assumed..."

"It's fine." He kissed her forehead. "I grew up in the wetlands just north of Amsterdam. She's a legit sex worker over there. I hear she's pretty good at her job. My mom never really wanted a kid. So she kept doing her thing and sent money to my grandparents, who raised me. We lived simply but had all the essentials. Unfortunately, my Opa had a massive brain aneurism and dropped dead while out in his garden one sunny afternoon. Not a bad way to check out, I guess. Oma didn't last too long after he'd passed. By the time I was fifteen, I was on my own. If I'd gone to my mother for help, I'm sure she would have done the right thing. But I figured a decade and a half of being bogged down financing another person's existence was enough punishment for a mistake or a fluke of biology, whatever I had been."

"No wonder you're so confident. You've always done things for yourself." She nuzzled his chest. "I admire that about you."

"Actually..." Tosin shook his head as he stared up at the ceiling. "I don't feel that way at all. It took me about two years of backpacking, wandering aimlessly with no home, no family, no purpose except to survive each day—and definitely no money—before I ran into Miguel and Archer. They became my family. Until them, I was pretty much a vagabond."

Tosin cleared his throat. Here came his biggest admission of all. "There were so many factors I had absolutely no control over that when it came to women and sex..."

"You like to be in charge," she simplified.

"I *need* it." He tried not to get turned on discussing this with her, considering her state. But imagining her peering up at him as she'd followed his directions earlier—sucking his cock so well, with enthusiasm if not skill—threatened to unleash another tsunami of desire within him. "The rush brings me satisfaction, yes. But the gift of a woman's surrender grounds me. Satisfying us both makes me sure that no matter what else happens, I have that part of my life in hand."

Kahori nodded slowly. She also squirmed against him, and he didn't think pain was responsible for her fidgeting this time.

"So that's why I'm curious." He hesitated until she looked at him. "Did you run from me because you liked the idea of sailing away with me, or did you run because you were afraid of the part of you that needs to submit?"

She took time to truly consider before whispering, "Both."

"Tell me more about the sex club you went to," he prompted.

"Ugh." She burrowed her face into his collarbone, hiding from him. "It was pretty much awful. Embarrassing and in no way enjoyable. It wasn't like the subtle way you took the lead before, which felt natural and honest to me."

Well, shit. That was going to make it a lot harder for him to admit he loved that sort of formal environment with established BDSM parameters. So much that he, Archer, and Miguel had their own private clubroom just down the hall. He would tell her, though, when she was ready to hear it and he was sure she wouldn't bolt again. If she stuck around that long.

First he had to know what he was up against.

"Did someone hurt you there?" He should have stopped devouring her in the cavern to have this discussion then, but he'd been too greedy and he'd paid the price for his avarice. Worse, so had Kahori. If he had done things the right way, maybe she never would have fled.

Instead, they'd be blissed out, probably lying on his blanket on the beach or enjoying the pineapple desserts back at island night.

The possibility that someone had raped her terrified him. He wasn't sure if he could overcome the deep scarring that such a violation could have left on her or if he was qualified to give her the support she would need if she had. He'd try his best, but maybe it wouldn't be enough.

She was quick to put him at ease, maybe underplaying things a little. "No. Nothing like that. It just was so contrived. There was no emotion. Completely opposite of what I felt with you tonight."

Kahori blushed as she admitted that, so he rewarded her with a careful kiss on her damaged lips. That tiny peck alone had him craving more. He stared into her eyes, scanning for any signs of discomfort, as he lingered there.

She practically purred and sank deeper into his sheltering embrace.

Perfect.

When they broke apart, she seemed stronger. She continued, "I convinced myself that if I was going to lose my V-card, it had to be then. I wasn't ready, but I wasn't going to have an opportunity again for who knew how long, so I picked someone who seemed decent enough to get the job done. Except when I realized the physical act alone wasn't going to satisfy my curiosity, I felt like I couldn't turn back. The guy—I didn't even know his name—held up his end of the bargain. He did as I asked and seemed to really get off on popping my cherry."

"Kahori, don't justify how he acted. He didn't do right by you." Tosin could see how she might think he had, though, if she'd never had a caring partner before. "Any man or woman has a responsibility to care for his or her partner. That shouldn't change just because you were at a club. I've fucked plenty of women casually. That doesn't mean I didn't take care of them, or honor their gift. Hell, I even think I gave them all the best parts of myself for that moment. That guy you were with should have seen it in your eyes, that you weren't really into it anymore. As the more experienced person, he should have cut you loose. He didn't. Selfish bastard."

"It would have been impossible for him to see my expression." She closed her eyes then, keeping Tosin from reading clues about her statement in them. He didn't care for that.

"What do you mean by that?" He noted the pounding of her pulse and the clenching of her hands as proof enough. If he could have kicked this guy's ass, he would gladly have done it. That loser *had* hurt her, even if she couldn't express the injury or admit it to herself.

"He put me on some kind of bench on all fours, with my ass in the air, then fucked me from behind." She winced then. "He said it would be less painful that way."

"That bastard lied to you." Tosin imagined how much deeper he could penetrate a lover in that position. He'd bet the guy hadn't been gentle either. He'd probably gotten off on impaling her on the first stroke, knowing no one had ever been deep in her pussy before.

Tosin had thought he'd reached a record level of anger earlier that night when he'd seen Kahori take a physical beating at the hands of a stranger. If he had, he shattered it again with a new high...or new low, depending on how you looked at it.

If he'd seen someone damaging Kahori that way, so much worse, he wouldn't have been able to stop himself from ripping their cock off with his bare hands to keep them from ever betraying a woman's trust so thoroughly again.

Tosin didn't bother asking if the fucker had at least taken time to get her off. It was clear he wasn't capable of that and she probably wouldn't have been able to climax after such rough treatment, even if he'd tried to take her there.

Then Kahori finished her story in a rush, as if expelling the last of the poison from a sea snake bite. "When he finished, he didn't even say goodbye. He walked away and left me there, wondering what the hell had just happened and how I could have been stupid enough to have thought this was what I wanted. A couple of strangers saw and helped me clean up the blood and get dressed."

"Wait." Tosin clenched his jaw. "He fucked you in a public space? Left you to fend for yourself after?"

"Yes. I'm kind of glad about that, actually, because those strangers were so kind. They tried to tell me not everyone there was like the guy I fucked. That if I came back they'd make it better. They drove me to my hotel, made sure I was okay. But I knew I'd never do it again. Despite what I thought, that kind of organized, artificial relationship isn't for me."

Tosin knew he'd have to respect her boundaries. Though she hadn't had a fair introduction to the kind of activities he sometimes indulged in, it would likely be a hard stop for her. And he would have to accept that if he wanted to spend more time with her. Show her how good sex could be with the right partner.

And he desperately wanted that. He'd never longed for something as badly as that in his life.

So he'd make sure she never knew that side of him or had a chance to mistakenly believe that he could be as callous as the person she'd had the misfortune to entrust with her virginity.

He'd make sure that the next time was the only time that counted.

Tosin held himself above her, careful not to apply pressure to any of her sore spots. He dropped his head and kissed Kahori, giving her a glimpse at how he'd be different from the only other man who'd been inside her. He'd ply her with anticipation, not fear. And hopefully, when their affair came to an end, he'd leave her with fond memories instead of regrets.

Fine cracks developed in his heart when he realized that it wouldn't be fair for him to talk about whisking her away from Aitutaki again. He wouldn't put her in that position—choosing between him and her father. Hell, they had a private jet. He could visit often. Or maybe even take a break from the *Divemaster* until they could figure something out.

Those were problems for another time.

For now, he only cared about taking away her pain and replacing it with something much sweeter. She sighed and touched his back, keeping him close to her. Hesitant at first, her inquisitive caresses turned into true embraces when he used his mouth and tongue to communicate just how much he enjoyed her touches.

One of her hands wandered from his shoulders to the dip of his waist. It crept lower, toward his ass. Meanwhile, he was careful to keep his pelvis far enough away that she couldn't feel how aroused he was by the strides they'd made, and her tentative affection.

Before he could get carried away, a knock came at the door and Archer called, "Can we come in?"

~ THIRTEEN ~

Kahori struggled to sit up, so Tosin rolled off her then lifted her shoulders, propping pillows behind them while she clutched the sheet to her chest. What was Pāpā going to have to say about seeing Tosin in bed with her and their clothes nowhere to be found?

This could be interesting.

Before she could bum a T-shirt off Tosin, he called, "Come in."

Except after Archer, Miguel, Waverly, Sabine, Banks, and Captain Alex piled into the room, making good use of the comfortable couch and pair of chairs in the seating area to the side of the bed.

"Pāpā?" Kahori asked.

Archer winced. "I'm sorry, we couldn't find him."

Kahori froze beside Tosin. Her breathing hitched and tears she hadn't shed for herself turned her eyes glassy. Had someone attacked him too? What was going on?

"Hey, hey. I'm sure there's an explanation. Maybe he's looking for you still?" Tosin didn't sound very sure as he attempted to reassure her.

It did seem pretty damn suspicious that he'd disappeared as soon as his daughter had been attacked. Kahori refused to believe that he'd somehow been involved. He would never do anything to put her in jeopardy.

"He was at the island night dinner," Tosin said to Archer. "Where the hell did he go?"

Miguel answered this time. "I was sitting right next to him arguing for the grow dome when we heard a faint scream. He shouted for Kahori, then took off sprinting toward her house. Most everyone else went in the other direction, heading for either the beach or the jungle. I know I did. So...no one's quite sure what happened to him after that."

Kahori didn't speak. Her vision blurred as flashbacks of the attack took center stage. "*Where is he? Where's the good stuff?* That's what they asked me. He couldn't mean Pāpā, could he?"

No one had answers for her. Unwilling to badmouth a man they'd never met, they let her make her own decisions on that front.

She looked up at Tosin then. He must have seen her fear in her eyes.

"Trust your gut, Kahori. Just because your mother cut you, that doesn't mean your dad stabbed you in the back." He'd nailed it. There was fear for Pāpā's safety, of course, but also fear of betrayal.

After tonight, she no longer knew what to believe when it came to other people.

Except that she trusted Tosin. She put her hand in his.

When she looked up, she noticed Banks's pinched expression. Oh shit, there was more?

Tosin gathered Kahori and lifted her gently onto his lap. He made sure he enveloped her in his arms as if they could provide some insulation against the next wave of agony that was about to get unleashed on her.

Eventually she realized that everyone was standing there, sober and quiet. Very unlike their usual chaotic state.

"Oh no. What else?" Kahori clung to Tosin like a black-lipped oyster's byssus adhered to the reef.

"I don't know if it was your dad or somebody else, but by the time we got to your house looking for him…" Archer shook his head. "Someone trashed your place. It seemed like they were looking for something. They went through your drawers and cabinets. Trashed your workshop. Your clothes, your bed…"

"We get the point," Tosin snapped, shooting Archer a *shut the fuck up* stare when Kahori began to quiver in his grasp.

"None of this makes sense!" She put her face in her hands for a few moments before gathering herself, striving for resilience. That was the only thing that was going to help them get to the bottom of this mess. "There's nothing of value in my house except my jewelry components—pearls and loose gems. Everyone on the island knows those are in a safe because of my insurance policy. It's kind of a running joke. I honestly only got the damn thing to protect against fires and floods, not because anyone would steal from me."

"That's pretty much what your cousin and uncle are telling everyone, too." Miguel clenched his fist. "It seems they're more in favor of believing us outsiders caused tonight's trouble. Hemi asked the council to kick us off the island. They voted down the grow dome and said they don't want our money or our problems."

"Oh no!" Kahori gasped. "That's ridiculous. Maybe I need to go back and straighten things out." She attempted to scoot out of bed, lack of clothes be damned.

Tosin refused to let her leave. "No way. Tonight has been fucked up enough as it is. We're safe on the *Divemaster*. You need to take it easy at least overnight."

"He's right, Kahori." Waverly jumped in then. "You scared the shit out of me on the flight back here. This mess can wait until tomorrow."

"In the morning, we'd be happy to take you home," Archer offered.

Tosin growled a warning.

"I don't think it's wise for you to stay there, but we'll escort you while you look around and see what's up. Maybe you can spot something we didn't notice." Banks suggested a middle ground. "For now, I think you should try to rest. Dr. Kleveno said it will do you a world of good. That's what your *pāpā* would want you to do, too."

She couldn't argue with that.

Another knock came at the door then followed by Dr. Kleveno asking, "Why does it sound like half the crew is in here?"

Captain Alex rushed to let her in despite the fact that she was probably going to ream them out for keeping Kahori awake. As if she could sleep now without knowing where her father was and what might have happened to him.

"Still doing okay?" Dr. Kleveno asked as she whipped out that insanely bright flashlight again.

When she rotated the end of the device to turn it on, the beam flashed across Sabine.

Kahori froze.

"Does that hurt?" Dr. Kleveno frowned. "If you're that sensitive to the beam from far away, you could have more damage than I suspected."

"Kahori?" Tosin asked her when she didn't respond right away.

She couldn't look away from Sabine. From there she couldn't be sure of what she'd seen. Maybe she *had* hit her head too hard. "Hey, can I see your earrings for a second?" She held her hand out to Sabine.

The other woman looked at her like Kahori definitely might have bonked the sense right out of her brain. She glanced at Miguel, who shrugged. Sabine slipped one from her ear, then tipped her head to start on the other.

"You can work later," Dr. Kleveno scolded Kahori. "I didn't mean for you to have so many visitors. It's best if you take it easy. Rest."

"Please. I need to see them." She shook her hand, palm up, curling her fingers toward her, completely ignoring the doctor's advice.

Sabine seemed unsure, but she passed over the earrings.

Immediately Kahori could tell something was off. "What did you do to these?"

"Nothing," the other woman swore. "I mean, I wore them today. That's it."

Kahori pointed to the jump rings that connected the pearls to the setting. "This isn't my work. These are sloppy. Look how the ends overlap and the circles are kind of squished out of shape. You're sure you didn't take them off and reattach them for some reason?"

"Why would she do that?" Banks asked.

"I have no idea." Kahori stared, looking from person to person, wondering exactly who she could trust. Her own eyes told her something was very wrong. Her new friends acted innocent. But if they hadn't tampered with her work, who had?

"Light." She waved for Dr. Kleveno to shine the torch directly on the earrings. Up close.

Kahori squinted at the overwhelming brightness. It was subtle but... "Something's not right with these. The luster is off."

Her heart rate tripled. She was an expert, someone who'd grown up around pearls and spent hours each day handling them, studying them, yet she could hardly tell. A common buyer would have no chance at spotting the inconsistencies here.

She pulled her lips back, grimacing at the sting, though it seemed to have lessened already. Kahori rubbed one of the pearls across her front tooth. It was gritty, as it should be. Fakes had a too-smooth surface compared to the natural nacre of a genuine pearl. At least poor fakes. To be sure...

"Sabine, do you have a microscope in your lab onboard?" Kahori wondered.

The other woman nodded.

"Would you mind terribly if I sacrificed one of these? I'll replace it." She was already shoving herself toward the edge of the bed. Besides, if what she suspected was true, they weren't worth anything anyway.

"Do whatever you need," Sabine said even as Dr. Kleveno and Tosin teamed up to keep Kahori in place.

"Hey, where do you think you're going?" he asked her, deep grooves marring his forehead.

"I need to see these under magnification." Kahori tried to tug free, but budging him was impossible. A rising tide of anxiety clawed up her insides. She tensed all over, causing her head to throb.

"No, what you *need* is to stay calm and still." Dr. Kleveno put her foot down. "You're not leaving this room."

"Hey, don't worry. I'll prep a slide for you." Sabine came nearer. She looked at the doctor, then Tosin, and lastly—when neither objected—to Kahori. "My microscope is digital. I'll email Tosin pictures. Will that work?"

"Yes, thank you." She relaxed against Tosin, just a little bit.

"Give me five minutes." Sabine reclaimed her earrings then left with Miguel on her heels.

The air seemed heavy. It made it hard to breathe. Kahori looked at Archer, who met her gaze directly. They had to be thinking the same thing. But it was impossible to tell him she was terrified the engagement ring he'd bought could have been tampered with too with Waverly standing right there.

So instead she plucked Tosin's hand from where it still cupped her upper arm. She drew it near and turned it over so that she could inspect the pearl clasp. She ran her thumb over the knot in the end of the leather. It wasn't as crisp as when she'd tied it.

Dread swamped her guts. "Light."

Dr. Kleveno shone the beam directly on the pearl. Kahori shoved Tosin's hand away before she could rip the bracelet from him and fling it against the wall. More of the same. What the hell was going on here?

Her panicked gaze flew to Archer.

He lifted his fingers at her in a subtle acknowledgement. "I'll be right back. Gotta take care of something quick."

Waverly asked, "Do you want me to come with you?"

He shook his head. "Stay in case they need you."

Kahori massaged the lump on the side of her head, which felt smaller but had started to ache and pulse as if it were dancing to the beat of the drums from earlier in the evening.

Dr. Kleveno took pill bottles from her purple satchel. Tosin held out a glass of water even as she shook a few capsules into her hand. "You'd better take these. We don't want to let your discomfort spiral out of control or it will be harder to manage and take longer to recover from."

Kahori was pretty damn sure her *discomfort* levels were about to shoot through the roof. Her father was missing. She'd gotten beat up. Her illicit liaison had ended in disaster. And now she suspected that she'd been unintentionally scamming innocent customers by selling them costume jewelry for top dollar.

Out of energy, she didn't argue, still trying to figure out how this could have happened and if it could be related to rest of the evening's events.

It had to be.

You can't fool us with our own tricks, they'd said.

When Tosin's phone bleeped, she couldn't seem to draw enough air into her lungs. He held it out to her, open to his email app. There were two messages from Sabine. The subjects were Sabine's Earrings and Waverly's Ring.

Oh God.

She selected the first message. It didn't take more than a glance at the close up to be sure. "They're junk. Not real."

"*What?*" Banks's eyebrows seemed like they were trying to join the hair on top of his head.

"The pearls in Sabine's earrings are manufactured. They're amazingly good fakes, but they're worthless. I'm so sorry." She clapped her hand over her mouth, trying not to look at Waverly.

Because if the earrings were phony, so was the clasp on Tosin's bracelet.

Kahori began to doubt everything she would have sworn to a minute ago.

The ring...

She'd handed it to Archer personally the other day after retrieving it from her safe. It had seemed exactly as she remembered. If it was phony too, she would never know how long she'd been unintentionally swindling her customers. Her business would be ruined along with her reputation.

It took her two tries to click the second email. When the microscope's enhanced image popped up, she sagged in relief.

The proper crystal structure—consistent yet disturbed periodically by natural imperfections not present in the manufactured version—was evident. It was real. She wasn't losing her mind.

"That one's good?" Tosin asked as he peeked over her shoulder.

She nodded. Then frowned. "The stuff from the Rarotonga shop is garbage. I need to talk to Hemi."

Even as she said it though, the room dimmed. It was too much. The day she'd had, complete with epic highs and lows. Her body couldn't take anymore. It started to shut down as if she was a nuclear reactor about to overheat.

"In the morning, Kahori." Tosin glanced at Dr. Kleveno, who nodded. "If you're up to it then, we'll take you over to the island to figure out what the hell is going on."

"Okay." She wished she could say more. As her medicine kicked in and numbness began to take away both her pain and her alertness, she tried again. "I'm sorry."

These people—and the rest of her clients, too—had no reason to believe she hadn't known what was happening beneath her nose. Hell, how hadn't she figured it out sooner?

There would be plenty of time for self-recrimination later.

With disgust, shame, and shock mixing into a super shot of misery, her mind could no longer function. From far away, she thought she heard Tosin encouraging her to relax by promising her everything would be okay.

She figured that was the only time since they'd met that he'd lied to her.

It seemed that was more than she could say for her own family.

Kahori went under."

Tosin kept his hand low on Kahori's back, not letting her out of his reach. Both to make sure she was steady on her feet and to remind himself that no one was actively threatening her.

She'd woken up bright and early, eaten a full breakfast, then refused to take any more painkillers, insisting she was sore but fine. He suspected she also intended to keep her mind fog-free so that they had no legitimate reasons to block her from assessing the damage at her house.

Her strategy had worked, though he'd had a hell of a time letting her leave the safety of the *Divemaster* without having a panic attack. They'd had enough near misses in the past year to put him on high alert. The rest of the crew, too.

So they were making a quick run, unannounced, over to her place. Then they'd have to figure out what came next based on anything they uncovered. The first batch of subjects in Sabine's trials were set to arrive in a few hours, along with Marta. Waverly would be shuttling them in, so she'd stayed behind also. The security on the ship had been beefed up in anticipation, but Captain Alex and Banks were both opposed to stretching their resources too thin.

Finally Tosin fully understood how hard it had been for Archer and Miguel when their women had been the ones threatened. Both guys shot him sympathetic looks as their tenders docked and they strode as quickly as possible toward Kahori's house.

"Hanging in there?" he asked her, wincing at their pace.

"Tosin, I promise I'm good." She flashed him a tight smile that called her a liar. More on the emotional side of things than the physical ones, he'd bet.

He squeezed her hand. "Keep in mind I give awesome piggyback rides, okay?"

"Will do." She smiled up at him, weak compared to her usually brilliant grin. Even that faded though when they reached her yard. Archer and Captain Alex went inside to scan the place while Banks, Miguel, and Tosin stayed on the porch with her.

"It's all clear," Archer announced when he returned. Then he winced. "Kahori, the place is a mess. Are you sure..."

"Yes." She put her hand on his chest and thanked him before pressing steadily until he backed out of her way.

Tosin loved that she wasn't a pushover. It would make her submission in bed worth even more to him than it already was.

To her credit, Kahori didn't flinch. She stepped over her ruined belongings, including the smashed jar and the flowers he'd given her yesterday, which were now dead. Ignoring her personal space, she made a beeline to her workshop and to the cabinet in the far back corner. When she opened the door, revealing her safe, she gasped. The door was covered with massive scrapes and dents that had obviously been caused by unsuccessful attempts to break into the locked box. Or a velociraptor.

"I'm guessing it didn't look like that yesterday?" Banks asked.

She shook her head then spun the dial until she'd entered the combination. Tosin never left her side. He rubbed her back as she yanked on the handle.

Inside, neat trays held pearls in graduated sizes. One rack was loaded up with glimmering jewels and precious metals. As if she didn't care that her inventory was still intact, she stayed tense. He realized why when she plucked a pearl at random then took it to her workbench and scoured the floor in search of her loupe.

When she had it in hand, she turned on some powerful gooseneck lamps and examined the pearl carefully. "It's real."

"Should we pack up the safe contents then?" Archer asked. "The *Divemaster* has secure facilities onboard for just this sort of thing. We installed them after we discovered a sunken treasure then sort of had part of it stolen temporarily."

Kahori gawked at him for a moment. Then she shrugged and laughed. "Sure, why not? I didn't realize you had experience in this sort of thing."

"Unfortunately," Miguel grumbled.

She paused then, growing much more serious. "I guess I'm lucky you all happened to come along when you did. I don't know what I would do right now if it wasn't for you. Thank you."

"We're happy to help." Tosin leaned in and kissed her cheek. "Now, is there anything else you want to check out or need to pack up? I don't think it's smart to hang out here any longer than necessary."

Kahori swallowed then, glancing around as if there would be a note from her dad telling her he'd gone out on a long fishing voyage or something equally as innocent. No such luck.

Instead, she wandered over to the opposite corner of the room then began to dig beneath a pile of crumpled invoices that had been dumped out of her filing cabinet. Beneath it all, in a tiny woven palm basket, she withdrew a plain brown paper covered package. "I hadn't finished weighing this one and putting the postage on before Pāpā took the rest of the orders to the post office on One Foot Island for me."

"Does he usually handle your shipments?" Archer asked.

"No, Hemi does. He runs the store on Rarotonga, too." She closed her eyes. "I thought he was just being helpful as always. But something was strange about it. On the way to island night I forgot my fire poi, and when I came back, Hemi was in here searching for the packages. Pāpā hadn't mentioned his mail run to Hemi even though he knows Hemi always takes care of that. Looking back..."

For the first time she wavered. Tosin was right by her side to hold her steady.

"I feel like the world's worst daughter for even considering that he could have done this. But besides that, the men in the jungle asked me where 'he' was. The only person missing is Pāpā. Nothing else makes sense, does it?" She hiccupped.

"While I hope you're wrong, I'm glad you're keeping your eyes open." Tosin rubbed her upper arms, which were chilled despite the heat. "And if it turns out that he did this, then I think it's *him* that's earned the title of world's worst."

"For shits and giggles..." Miguel looked to Tosin, then Kahori. "I think you should open that. If they're real too, then maybe the switcheroo is happening on Rarotonga. Maybe it's Hemi we should be worried about."

Kahori looked ill. She plopped into her office chair as if the thought hadn't occurred to her. "They're my family. I can't believe we're even having this discussion. Besides, Hemi was at the island night the entire time last night, right?"

Banks nodded. "I was sitting right next to him when everything went to hell."

She turned the package over in her hands a few times before psyching herself up. When she grabbed a letter opener from a tipped earthen cup and went to slice the packing tape, she froze. "It's been tampered with. I can see two layers of tape already."

As if she still didn't want to believe, she practically stabbed the package then ripped it open. A pearl necklace poured into her hand. Kahori took one look at it and began to sob. She grasped the strand in each of her hands and yanked, snapping it in half.

Fake pearls rained on the floor among the rest of the rubble.

Tosin rushed to her and crouched by her feet. He hugged her, guiding her face to his shoulder as she cried.

"Pāpā! Pāpā, why?" She broke their hearts as she expelled her misery.

No one had an answer to that question except her father. And he was definitely missing. Either he'd realized they were on to him and he'd run, abandoning his daughter to madmen…or they'd gone after him too, and he hadn't been as lucky as Kahori.

When her bawling had slowed to weeping, Banks and the rest of the guys huddled around. "We really should get moving." Banks told them.

"But where?" Kahori asked. "You said it yourself, the ship has a lot going on right now. I won't endanger anyone else over my family's problems."

The guys winced. They'd like to argue, but the reality was they couldn't take chances anymore. They'd learned from past mistakes and wouldn't put anyone at risk.

"Look, we only need to buy a little time." Archer told her. "As soon as we're back to the *Divemaster*, Captain Alex and I will meet with the security team. Banks can have reinforcements flown in from New Zealand. It can probably be done in the next twenty-four hours. Where can we hide you until then?"

Tosin suggested, "How about the glowworm cavern? I'm staying with you. We can hide out there pretty comfortably for a while."

"I have a better idea." She wiped her eyes on the sleeve of the shirt she'd borrowed from Sabine. "Do you trust me?"

"Absolutely."

Kahori appreciated Tosin holding her hand for the entire boat trip over to the *motu* that housed her uncle Kimo's resort. Even that simple connection was enough to stabilize her. In the end, Archer and Miguel had decided to stay with them while Captain Alex and Banks returned to the ship to make the arrangements they'd agreed to.

Archer drove while Miguel searched the ocean around them with a pair of high-tech binoculars. Every minute or two he checked in with the head of their security detail back on the *Divemaster*.

They glided along outside the barrier reef, staying out of sight as much as possible before she directed Archer to duck through a slit in the coral on the backside of the *motu*. It was less than a minute before they had beached the rigid hull inflatable boat with its ridiculously overpowered engine then hauled it into the trees where it practically vanished from view.

The men walked in a triangle, keeping her at the center.

It felt so strange to be this cautious. To worry in a place that had only ever been peaceful before. The loss of that purity nearly shattered her again. Instead, she put her shoulders back and marched through the open-air lobby of Uncle Kimo's resort and into his office.

He stood as they entered, a spear gun in his hands. When he recognized her, he propped it in the corner then flew to her side. Tosin stepped in front of her, blocking her uncle from invading her space.

"Because I appreciate what you did for her, I won't hold that against you, *papa'a*. But I suggest you move now so I can see my niece." Kimo spoke softly. The *tā moko*—decorative scarring around his eyes and along his jaw—he wore gave his underlying threat some heft, too.

Still, Tosin didn't budge.

"It's okay." Kahori touched his arm softly. So he relented and let the man pass. When Kimo carefully enfolded her in his embrace, Tosin relaxed.

"I can't believe this is happening." Hearing the disbelief and pain in her gruff uncle's voice made Kahori feel better about how she'd broken down in her workshop.

"You're hurt. Ruru is missing." At the mention of his brother, Kimo let Kahori go then pounded his fist on his desk hard enough to rattle everything on it. "What the hell is going on?"

"We're not sure yet." Kahori glanced at Tosin. He shrugged, leaving it to her discretion to confide in Uncle Kimo or not. They had to start asking some questions to find the answers they needed. This was as good a place as any to start.

"But you have some clue?" Kimo narrowed his eyes.

Kahori told him about the fake pearls and how they suspected the brutes who'd chased her had been some sort of collection crew that her father may have attempted to double-cross.

"They'll be back." Kimo sagged against his desk. "You can't go home, Kahori."

"I know." She considered how he might take the news of the rest of their plan. In the end, she divulged everything. If she trusted her family and that ended up being the wrong call, she'd have to accept the consequences. But mistrusting even the people who'd loved her most seemed like a greater crime. "These guys are going to help me out. They've got more security coming in first thing in the morning. Until then, I was hoping Tosin and I could hide out in the honeymoon suite. Archer and Miguel will stay too, to guard the entrance."

Her uncle frowned at first. Thinking of his gorgeous niece and a foreigner in the same sentence as "honeymoon suite" probably didn't sit well, though as the island's resort owner he certainly had more exposure to visitors, which had softened his traditional views. Eventually, he relented. "You're right. It's the easiest spot to protect. Since there's only one way in..."

Kahori thought about the overwater cabana. It would be like a mini fort. No one could sneak up on them. "That's what I was thinking, too."

"Go ahead, Kahori. The longer we talk, the more likely it is someone might see you." He shooed her. When she turned around, Hemi stood—feet spread, thick arms crossed—blocking the doorway.

"You're letting them stay here?" He spat the question as if it were an accusation.

"She's family—of course. Your uncle Ruru would do the same for you if something happened to me." Kimo gestured for his son to move.

He didn't.

The three divemasters huddled around her like a living, breathing shield.

"See…here you are inviting them in when they probably killed Uncle Ruru and fed him to the sharks," Hemi snarled, viciously enough that spittle launched from his ruddy face.

"Right now you seem more violent, and far less civilized, than our guests." Uncle Kimo put Hemi in his place.

"*I* can take care of Kahori." Hemi bucked against his father's authority. "We don't need them."

"If Tosin goes, so do I," Kahori objected at the same time Tosin simply said, "No."

"I never expected you to be the sort to choose a *papa'a* over your own blood." Her cousin scanned her appraisingly. Then he shrugged. "Have it your way."

Then he retreated to the check-in desk, where he answered a ringing phone, speaking quietly into the receiver as if he hadn't been shouting moments earlier.

Kahori thanked her uncle then edged out the door toward the honeymoon suite.

"*Tamāhine*," Uncle Kimo called for his niece. "Ignore my foolish son. He is hurting too. Don't lose hope. Your *pāpā* is coming back. He would never choose to leave you. Understood?"

"Yes, uncle." She wished the sickness in her gut didn't say otherwise.

⁀ SIXTEEN ⁀

Kahori waved Archer and Miguel inside when they hesitated on the threshold. She knew why.

Because the honeymoon suite was clearly a place designed for romance. The overwater cabana had multiple decks complete with loungers and even a splash pool. Inside, it was a whole new level of cozy. Entire walls were made of glass. Gauzy fabric billowed around a giant four-poster bed. Flowers overflowed vases around the room.

For nearly everyone who stayed here, it was a once-in-a-lifetime way to commemorate the happiest days of their life. A new start with their soul mate.

"You guys can keep watch from in here." Kahori smiled. "No reason to be uncomfortable. Besides, you'll be less visible if you stay inside."

Of course the three divemasters were already peering off the edge of the deck into the shallow water below. She didn't blame them. A gorgeous reef sat in about twenty feet of water, drawing a million colorful creatures.

Miguel elbowed Tosin. "You hear that? No nookie for you. We're your roomies for the night."

"Fuck you," Tosin grumbled.

Archer laughed at them both.

Kahori had other plans. She took Tosin's hand, loving how large and strong it felt cupping hers. Even better, she was excited that she might be able to do something amazing for him. Give him an experience that even his millions might not have bought him yet. "Don't worry, Tosin. You'll have the last laugh tonight."

"Ohh, a peep show?" Miguel asked. "I'll have to text Sabine and see if I'm allowed to watch."

"Not exactly." Kahori patted him on the shoulder. "Don't be too jealous, okay?"

That got the guys' attention. All three of them stared at her as she wandered toward what appeared to be a glass-topped table in the center of the room.

Kahori grabbed a handle hidden on the underside then lifted. The top pivoted open, revealing a hatch and a ladder going down.

Tosin's eyes grew wide as he rushed to her side and peered into the space below. Instead of ocean waves, a richly appointed room inside what was essentially a giant glass bubble awaited. "Is that for real? An underwater bedroom?"

"Why don't you check it out and see for yourself?" She smiled then waved him toward the space usually reserved for the resort's most extravagant customers.

He didn't hesitate another moment. Tosin clambered down the ladder so fast it might as well have been a fireman's pole. He ignored the high-end finishes of the unique bedroom to stare at the ocean surrounding them through the transparent walls of the suite. "It's like I can finally breathe underwater. Pretty much my biggest fantasy. Well, you know, other than the sex kind."

"I suppose that's true." She hopped to the ground, happy when her ribs and skull only protested the jarring maneuver a tiny bit. "Best of all, no one can sneak up on us down here. Hell, they're not likely to find us even if they raid the cabana."

From above, Miguel and Archer were cursing their best friend. Miguel tried to bribe his way inside. "Dude, I'll give you a million dollars if you switch places with us."

"Make it two million." Archer didn't sound like he was joking either.

"Sorry, boys, you'll have to try some other time. We're all booked up for tonight." Tosin waved cheekily at his partners. "Close the door—er, table—would you?"

"Have fun, lucky bastard," Miguel said then did as asked.

The second the sound from above was eliminated, the room seemed like a giant people bowl—you know, an aquarium where they were on display for the entertainment of the fish around them. Kahori had loved this room as a child. Hell, she still did now.

"I could stay here forever." Tosin wandered to an oversized window seat that was really more of a spacious divan. He stretched out on it then patted the space in front of him.

Kahori joined him. When she neared, he reached for her, wrapping his arm around her waist then drawing her down in front of him so that they were both lying on their sides, her head pillowed carefully on his biceps as they stared at the butterfly fish schooling beyond the glass.

"If everything wasn't so shitty outside right now, I'd say this was heaven. You, this place...I've got everything I need right here," he murmured close to her ear as he curled around her.

"I need a break, Tosin. Until tomorrow, can we leave everything but us and this beauty out there? Forget it exists?" She ran her fingers along the arm he'd tossed over her waist.

"That sounds like the best idea I've heard in a while." He kissed her cheek then acted like the only important thing in the world was them and their connection. He asked, "What's your favorite sea creature?"

Kahori was happy to play this game with him.

"Easy. *Pā'ua*. I think you call them giant clams." She pointed at one of the most beautiful examples she'd ever seen, nestled at the base of the reef about ten feet away from where they were laying. The enormous mollusk shell was impressive, but the mantle of neon blue and green photosynthetic material was easily the most unbelievable and stunning thing she'd ever seen in nature. It didn't look real. "That one is about four feet wide. It's lived here for at least seventy-five years. My grandfather wrote about it in his journal. It was one of the reasons Uncle Kimo chose this spot for the honeymoon suite."

"Good choice. They're awesome." He hugged her as tight as possible without causing her bruised skin any discomfort. "Unfortunately, they're also endangered."

Not so different than her these days.

No, she would not let those thoughts intrude.

For a very long time they simply enjoyed each other's company, pointing out the interesting things—like a manta ray, and a massive travally, and even a few black-tipped reef sharks—that wandered past their outpost. The constant swirl of color and life mesmerized them both.

As fascinating as the scenery was, Kahori eventually couldn't stand facing away from the one thing she most wanted to see. She rolled over in Tosin's arms so she could study his face. His eyes were even more striking since they reflected the turquoise water surrounding them. "You know, this isn't called the honeymoon suite for nothing. It would be a shame to pass up an opportunity like this..."

Tosin leaned in to kiss her. The brush of his lips was even gentler than it had been the first time he'd tasted her. So she knew he was holding back.

Though she understood his concern, she couldn't help but be kind of insulted that he didn't think her tough enough to handle him. "Lame, Tosin."

He barked out a laugh. "Sorry. I'm afraid I'll hurt you. Or frighten you. Why don't you let me hold you again tonight? I enjoyed the hell out of that last night and we didn't even have this view to entertain us."

"Not good enough." Kahori hoped he didn't call her on that whopper. She would be satisfied with his comforting embrace in this ultra-peaceful haven if that was all they could muster. But she knew they were capable of a lot more than that.

And if this was her one chance, she didn't want to waste it like she had during their time in the cave. If only she'd stayed, maybe none of this would have happened.

Maybe her father wouldn't be missing.

Maybe she wouldn't have been brutalized.

"You want me to make love to you?" he asked.

She nodded. "Please."

"I'm warning you, Kahori. If we have sex tonight...here, in this magical place, with my emotions so wild already, and it being essentially your first time—the first time that counts, as far as I'm concerned—well, I can't be responsible for what happens."

"They're just a few bruises, nothing major. You're not going to hurt me if you get carried away," she reassured him.

"That's not what I meant." He sighed then kissed her again, deeper this time. "If we do this, I'm going to fall in love with you. Hell, I'm halfway there already. Are you sure you want me following you around begging for your attention for the rest of your life?"

She laughed.

Except maybe he wasn't kidding.

"I haven't said those words to anyone since my grandparents passed away, Kahori. You're the first person who's made me even consider exposing myself to that kind of complication. I'm loyal, or stubborn—your call. Once my mind is made up, I'm not going to change it. So be sure that you really want me too—for more than a solid fuck—before you spread your legs for me."

How could he say something so nasty, so crude, yet make it seem so romantic?

She didn't understand, but that didn't keep her from swooning a little inside.

That was what she'd thought she was signing up for when she'd gone to that club.

"Count me in. I've waited forever for this moment, Tosin. Now I know I was waiting for you." Kahori pounced then, clasping his head in her hands, loving the brush of his short blond hair against her palms. She held him still as she advanced, then devoured him thoroughly.

Until he turned the tables on her.

∽ SEVENTEEN ∽

Kahori obeyed the pressure of Tosin's hands, which guided her into a kneeling position, straddling his narrow waist. He smiled up at her as he grabbed the hem of her shirt then lifted it. She accommodated him by putting her arms up and hunching forward to allow the material to slide off.

Braless, her breasts were on display for him.

Coconut bras didn't go well beneath shirts, even if she'd been able to salvage the ruined one from the night before. Fortunately, or maybe unfortunately for Tosin, she was more pert than plump.

He didn't seem to mind.

His hands landed on her waist, his thumbs brushing low on her belly, making her squirm. Of course that only rubbed her pussy over the front of his shorts and the thick erection waiting beneath.

"Are you sure you're up for this?" he asked as he skimmed upward until he lightly traced the outline of the purple discoloration on her breast, an unpleasant reminder of the day before. He brushed his lips over the area as if he could kiss it and make it better.

Maybe he could.

It sure as hell felt fine when he did that.

"Yes." She let her eyes fall closed for a moment as he amused himself with her body. "I'll beg if you really want me to."

"I'm not opposed." The gravelly rasp his voice picked up then made her smile.

"Please Tosin, take me. Make me yours." She shrieked then giggled when he growled. His hands cradled her as he lifted her and rotated all at once.

Kahori wasn't entirely sure how he managed it without dumping both their asses on the floor, but next thing she knew she was gazing up at him as he rid her of her skirt and himself of his own clothes. While he did, he removed another condom from his pocket and rolled it down his hard-on.

Too bad—she would have enjoyed tasting him again.

She licked her lips.

"Don't worry, you're going to have me inside you soon." He dropped low over her to kiss her, then asked, "That's what you want, isn't it? Me fucking you, slow and deep?"

Uh huh. Yep. That sounded about right.

"Tell me, Kahori." He brushed the pad of his thumb over her mouth. "Invite me inside you."

"I want to feel you pressing into me, locking us together." She practically panted then. "Please Tosin, give me your cock."

"Oh fuck, you're a little too good at naughty talk." He strangled his cock then stroked a few times, as if he couldn't help touching himself because of her and her dirty desires. "But I think I can make you beg even more prettily next time."

She didn't understand what he meant until she realized he was sinking between her legs. Not hips to hips, though. No, he was shoving her legs wide to accommodate his shoulders.

"You should have known I wasn't going to dive right in without eating this pretty pussy again first." He licked her from the bottom of her slit to her clit.

Kahori didn't plan to argue. She arched her back and spread her legs farther open, giving him room to work.

"That's right." He hummed as his mouth settled over her pussy and began to reward her for being bold.

It was every bit as spectacular as the day before. Maybe more so because now she was certain that this was only the appetizer to a banquet. She planned to feast—on Tosin.

He'd made her come a few times, asking her again if she wanted his cock following each orgasm. When her begging didn't motivate him to fuck her, he started over again with his mouth.

So this time, when he wiped his lips on the back of his hand, smirked, then said, "How badly do you want my cock now?" Kahori writhed on the divan. She lunged for his erection, which bobbed just out of reach.

Then a stream of utter depravity she never would have believed herself capable of poured out of her. "I'll do anything to have you inside me. Please, Tosin, give me your cock. My pussy aches. Fill me up so that I never again feel empty or alone."

"That's better." He grinned, though it turned soft and affectionate pretty quickly.

"You do the same for me, you know. Make me feel fully engaged with life." He kissed her softly then, aligning their bodies. Finally, finally, he was going to show her what she'd been missing.

Kahori held her breath as if they truly swam beneath the surface of the ocean that surrounded them. Funny enough, she in no way felt like she was drowning when Tosin levered himself over her carefully. Instead, she felt more like she was flying, or could take off soon.

"I want to make up for everything that other guy did wrong with you," he murmured.

"You already have." She hugged him, hoping she never had to let go.

"You should know this is different for me, too." He kissed the tip of her nose. "I've gotten so used to emotion-free fast fucks I'm not sure I'm going to be any good at this kind of sex."

Could he seriously doubt that? "I'm going to go out on a limb and say you'll do just fine."

Tosin threw back his head and laughed. He pinched her nipple teasingly. "You're lucky I'm too horny to put you over my knee right now."

Was she? Kahori shivered. Because the thought of his hand on her bare ass turned her on even more. Something she never would have expected.

"If you look at me like that any longer while you're thinking about me turning that ass red, I might shoot before I get inside you." He growled, then nipped her neck. "Are you ready for me, Kahori? Ready to seal this deal?"

"Do it." She grabbed his hips, her fingers splaying across the upper swells of his tight ass.

When he advanced, the tip of his sheathed cock prodding the opening to her body, she was grateful for the time he'd taken to warm her up. He glided through the slick furrow of her pussy, coating himself in her natural lubrication.

Then he pressed down on his cock with two fingers, aiming himself properly as he began to sink inside her, penetrating every last barrier she'd erected to protect her heart from being stolen.

Unlike last time, there was no sting, no burn, no stabbing white-hot poker between her legs.

Instead, there was only pleasure.

Tosin worked himself within her clinging sheath so carefully she thought she might go crazy before she could come on his shaft. When he was finally fully seated, he kissed her, then asked, "Still good?"

"Amazing." She wrapped her legs around his waist and tried to draw him in tighter with her heels.

"You've got all of me," he promised her.

Kahori swallowed hard, overwhelmed by emotions. She touched his face lovingly with the tips of her fingers. And then he began to move.

Slowly at first. With liquid glides that caressed her from the inside. He rode her with measured strokes that inspired her to think of new and filthier ways to beg him to make her come. The persistent drilling of his cock and the stroking of his fat head near the entrance of her pussy eventually proved too much.

His careful probing turned to something less restrained. And when he cursed, then scooped his hands beneath her shoulders to brace her against the increasing tempo and pressure of his thrusts, she knew she'd gotten to him too.

Tosin hunched his back so he could suckle her nipple as he began to dig deep on every forward pass. He brought all of her most sensitive places to life. Of course her pussy and her breasts, plus everywhere they rubbed skin on skin. Even better, he began to restore her faith in men and in the benefits of a true physical and emotional connection with a sexual partner.

"You're almost there, aren't you?" He smiled as if nothing could make him happier than delivering bliss to her.

"Yes. So close." She rocked her head from side to side as her hips lifted, trying to bury him to the hilt within her.

Too late—he was already as deep as he could get.

Tosin picked up the pace again, this time pressing his body against her clit and swiveling his hips just a bit at the apex of each thrust. But it was when she opened her eyes and looked directly into his that she knew she had lost everything—her heart most of all—to him.

"That's right, let me have your first orgasm with a man. Squeeze my cock with that tight pussy. Show me how much better this is. How perfect."

Kahori had no idea how he could still talk. She opened her mouth, but all that came out was a scream right as her climax struck. Her pussy strangled Tosin's dick and he joined her, pumping his release into the condom keeping them just the tiniest bit separate.

Next time she'd convince him to remove the last of the barriers between them, though she wasn't sure it could feel any better than this without killing her in the process. Her heart galloped wildly, her pussy clenched, wringing his cock dry, and euphoria spread into every cell of her body.

Utterly content, she collapsed onto the divan, welcoming the weight of Tosin's equally drained body lying on top of her. They dozed then fucked then dozed some more. The entire night passed in a blur of passion and discovery she would never forget.

The next morning, soft blue light filtered through the shallow water and illuminated their hidey-hole. Kahori leaned her back against Tosin's chest. He had her wrapped in his arms and legs, utterly secure in his embrace. They didn't speak as they watched the ever-evolving aquatic landscape swirling around them.

After last night, what would happen now?

Part of her felt guilty for having the best night of her life while her father was missing. Another part swam in gratitude that Tosin had reminded her the world held as much beauty as pain. Kahori was terrified to leave this place knowing their bubble would burst and the peaceful intermission they'd crafted for themselves would end.

Starving, she couldn't stay down here much longer without going in search of breakfast. Tosin's stomach was growling too. Yet instead of acknowledging it, he only rubbed his cheek against the crown of her head and held her tighter against him.

Until something in her peripheral vision caught her attention.

"Is that—?" Kahori started to ask at the same time Tosin waved.

A second diver joined the first she'd spotted. They descended until they were level with the bed and Kahori and Tosin's very naked bodies.

"Oh my God!" Kahori dove under the comforter. "Miguel! Archer!"

Tosin cracked up, giving her ass a playful swat before ensuring she was covered. "You know, there are plenty of times we make the *Divemaster* clothes-optional. There's no need to hide if you don't want."

The divemasters waved from outside the glass enclosure. Miguel tugged a slate from a retractable cord on a carabiner attached to his buoyancy control device. He drew something quick then turned it around so she could read what he'd written.

Good morning! Did you miss us? Extra security is here, watching your door for us, was surrounded by hearts, flowers, and a big-ass smiley face.

"You know the only way to prank a prankster is to one-up them, right?" Tosin asked her as she snickered.

"Then I guess you'd better get over here and give them a show," Kahori responded as liquid heat filled her belly. Who would have thought the idea of being watched surrendering to Tosin would turn her on?

It did.

In the end, they had the last laugh...and a pair of orgasms to go with it.

When Kahori remembered where she was and opened her eyes, the men had disappeared. She didn't care. Only one man mattered. Then and always.

It would always be Tosin.

"I warned you last night, didn't I?" He gazed down at her as he disengaged himself from her body.

She blinked up at him.

"I love you, Kahori."

What he hadn't said then, or now, was that it wasn't only him who had been affected. She'd been trapped just as surely and it was impossible to regret it even if she couldn't take it back.

"I love you, too."

"Thank God." He groaned. "Now, can we please find something to eat before I'm reduced to gnawing on my own arm or something? I'm dying."

Kahori slapped his shoulder then laughed. "You did work up quite an appetite, didn't you?"

"Mmmhmm." He looked at her as if he might consider eating her again instead, then sighed. "You ready?"

"No, but at least I know you'll be with me." She put her hand in his.

"Always." Tosin took one last lingering look around the underwater room. "You think Archie will let me install a giant glass panel somewhere in the *Divemaster's* hull?"

"Doesn't hurt to ask, huh?" She would love to recreate the best experience of her life. "If he does, I want a do-over."

"Deal."

∽ EIGHTEEN ∽

With their enhanced security in place, Tosin, Kahori, Archer, and Miguel didn't dally before heading home to the *Divemaster*. Archer hated being away from the ship during such an important transition, and Miguel seemed half-excited, half-terrified to meet the woman who was as close to an in-law as he'd probably ever have.

He shouldn't have worried. Marta greeted them along with the rest of their friends when they charged up the gangway into their waiting, open arms. Relieved hugs were exchanged all around.

It felt nice to have them to return to when all that was left for Kahori on the island was a ruined home or becoming an obligation for her uncle to take care of. Before she could depress herself with thoughts like those, or worry about her *pāpā*, she'd been whisked off for a checkup by Dr. Kleveno.

Tosin had some dives to do with the family members of Sabine's trial patients, so Kahori found herself wandering, alone, after a while. When she stumbled on a lovely seating area beside the pool, she curled up in a lounger and took a nap since Tosin hadn't let her do much sleeping the night before.

Kahori yawned and stretched some time later. Soft voices drifted to her on the light breeze. She blinked and scrubbed her eyes seeing Marta and Sabine not far away. She was about to get up and join them when she realized their posture was slightly tense, so she listened before approaching.

Marta took Sabine's hand. "Do you think this is right? Especially so soon? It's only been six months since Heinrich left us. Would he be upset with me?"

"For loving someone else? A very decent, generous, and devoted person?" Sabine hugged Marta. "Never. He would have hated for you to be lonely."

"You know no one will ever replace him in my heart, right?" Marta asked.

"Of course," Sabine whispered. "I'm sure Banks understands that too. Remember, I lost my parents, but that didn't stop you and Heinrich from taking up the job where they left off. There's room enough to love an infinite number of people in our lifetimes. We should do that. You two taught me that."

Kahori didn't mean to eavesdrop. Neither did she want to shatter such a critical and dear moment between the two women. Unfortunately, their unconditional support and sage advice got to her. She sniffled.

Marta looked over and smiled. "Oh, hello, sleepyhead. Feeling better now?"

Kahori nodded. "I'm sorry to interrupt, I just..." She waved at her chair and then to them.

"Join us for a moment, would you?" Marta asked.

Kahori respected her elders, so of course she didn't decline. She slipped into an empty seat at the table where the women were sipping iced tea. They poured her a glass as well.

"I'm very sorry to hear about your father." Marta put her hand over Kahori's and squeezed.

Kahori couldn't speak, and not because of the giant gulp she'd taken of her drink in an attempt to swallow the fear that kept rising up within her.

"I know it's hard—we both do—losing someone so important in your life, whether in a tragedy or because you have to find your own way. But I think most parents would agree that they want their children to grow into the best versions of themselves. To venture beyond what was possible for themselves. I don't know you yet, honey. And I may never meet your father. But it was obvious to me after a moment or two, that you've found your future with Tosin. I'd think awfully hard before throwing that away. Sometimes you don't get a second chance."

Kahori agreed. *When* her *pāpā* came home, she would talk to him about Tosin and the changes she needed to make in her life to be happy regardless of how things turned out with the sexy divemaster.

"And that's all I'm going to say about that." Marta smiled then hugged Kahori.

The women moved on, discussing everything from jewelry to experiment results to favorite destinations. She'd never had these kinds of independent female role models growing up. But now that she saw how strong and career minded Waverly and Sabine were, and the way their guys supported them, Kahori had a new goal.

Restless as she considered how to broach the topic with Tosin, she excused herself from Marta and Sabine then wandered the ship. Every place she turned, there was something amazing she'd never seen before. And when she was nearly back to Tosin's room, where she planned to wait for him to finish his session—anytime now—she noticed Waverly and Archer slipping into that funny black door she'd wondered about on several occasions.

It didn't quite shut behind them, so she hurried to catch up.

"Hey, Archer. If you're back, does that mean Tosin is finished too?" She poked her head in the door, which she realized had been kept open by Waverly's bra lodged in the opening.

Things only got more bizarre from there.

The interior of the space looked nothing like the rest of the ship.

Dark leather chairs that looked almost like thrones faced an open area dotted with black-painted equipment. She recognized a St. Andrew's cross, a suspension harness, and—worst of all—a spanking bench like the one she'd been forced to bend over at the club on her disastrous outing.

Waverly and Archer were already pressed up against some contraption she couldn't make sense of as they tore at each others' remaining clothes.

Holy shit.

Kahori squeaked in surprise.

Both of them whipped around to look at her. Surprisingly, neither seemed very upset to see her there.

"Hey." Archer grinned. "Did you and Tosin have the clubroom booked? I'm not going to lie, I didn't bother to look at the schedule when Waverly propositioned me."

"Tosin? Clubroom?" she stammered.

"Uh oh." Waverly nabbed her shirt off the floor and flung it haphazardly over her nakedness.

"Fuck." Archer was already on the move. He hit an intercom on the wall and said, "Tosin. Clubroom. Right fucking now. Kahori is here."

"Don't let her leave until I get there," came the immediate reply.

Not... "Hey, what's a clubroom?"

Or... "Why would she be in there? I hate that kind of thing."

Or anything else that would alleviate the betrayal and fear bubbling up within her.

∾ NINETEEN ∾

Tosin didn't dally. Neither did he run.

More than ever before in his life, it was critical that he stay calm and handle the situation carefully. Prove to Kahori that not everyone who enjoyed structured playtime would disregard the needs of their submissive partner.

He had to believe that, deep down, she knew that already.

It was his job to unlock her emotions, and smother her fear, so that her brain could catch up with the rest of her.

When he reached the clubroom's onyx door, his hand hovered over the handle. He was surprised to see it trembling. It was too late now to pray that he hadn't gone about this all wrong.

Tosin drew in a deep breath, then opened the door.

"You liar!" Kahori ripped free of Archer's light restraint and flew at him, her fists pounding on his chest. "You're into the same things as that guy at the club. At least he didn't try to lure me in with pretty words and gentle sex before showing me what he really liked."

"I never deceived you, Kahori." He kept her from assaulting him by braceleting her wrists with his thumbs and forefingers. He didn't apply a lot of pressure. Didn't need to. She responded to him beautifully as always, completely in tune with his intentions.

"How can you say that? You listened to me confess about that club. How contrived it was, how unappealing to me. And yet this... You went to enormous lengths to have a place like this onboard so it must be important to you! Why waste your time on me or make me fall for you when you knew we're interested in two totally different things?" She railed at him and he let her get it all out before explaining what he'd been attempting to do. "Here I was, feeling guilty about fucking you when I can't leave my home, abandon my *pāpā*, and the whole time you were hiding...*this*!"

Archer shook his head—probably mentally labeling Tosin an idiot for that kind of supposed gaff— then snuck out the door with Waverly, shutting it gently behind him.

"You weren't ready for this." Arrogant, maybe. But it was the truth. "From what I've seen so far, you haven't yet accepted that you enjoy being topped by a responsible lover. You don't understand the subtleties of the relationship because of very valid fears. I was working on showing you the more subtle flavors first before I asked you to try something the equivalent of mainlining hot sauce."

"What the hell is that supposed to mean?" She propped her hands on her hips, practically daring him to enlighten her. So he did.

"Remember in the cave, when I instructed you how to blow me? Or in the underwater lodge, how hard you came on my cock when I commanded you to?" He would never forget it. "You like letting go. Giving me complete control. But you don't know me well enough to look beyond your history with a dumbass, reckless user who doesn't know how to treat a prized partner to realize that with someone else, it would be a different experience entirely."

Kahori had gone silent.

"A power exchange doesn't have to be this blatant. There are lots of shades to enjoy on the spectrum of BDSM. I was simply trying to figure out what colors would be our favorites together. But if you'd like to test my theory about which hues you'll come to love, I'm happy to try that out, too."

"Who are you?" She squinted, as if trying to detect some hidden marking on him that would have declared his alpha tendencies.

"The same man you claimed to love." He held his hand out to her. "We've hardly met. You can't think you know all of me yet. I'm certain I've only scratched your surface. But if you like, I'll introduce you to another side of me."

"Why do you keep speaking in riddles?" She wasn't saying no. She also wasn't leaving despite the clear path to the exit. He took that as a good sign, both that she was interested, and that she wasn't freaking out.

Deep down, she knew he would never hurt her. She trusted him enough to hear him out.

That had to be a good sign.

Tosin wanted nothing more than to reward her bravery and be the man she didn't even know she so desperately needed. He smiled at her, hoping she could see that enjoying what went on in this room didn't detract from the genuine devoted exchanges they'd had outside of it. "Sometimes sweet is sexy. But sometimes I like going hard. I think you'll like it a hell of a lot too if you give it a chance. You were interested enough to check it out on your own. But I think you might not have understood that any sex can be good sex with the right person or a disaster if you don't have a true partner."

Kahori wrung her hands in front of her. She took a tiny step closer to him.

So he held out his hand to her and asked, "Will you let me show you?"

"Will you stop if I realize it's honestly not for me?" Her eyes begged him so prettily as she asked, though she must already know the answer.

"Of course. Would you like a safe word?" He rubbed his palms up and down her arms, chasing away the goose bumps there as she proved yet again how spectacular she was and how strong their bond had grown in a matter of a few intense days. "If you say it, at any time, everything stops. I'll take you out of here and we don't ever have to mention it again. Believe it or not, with you, I don't *need* this. We have something harder to find. This is a means to an end, a shortcut where everyone understands the rules. What you and I were building was something more intricate, more subtle, and...well, just *more* in every way."

Kahori squeezed her eyes shut as she considered what he was offering. Then she opened them and stared directly at him as she nodded.

"Thank you for trusting me." He held his arms open and she flew into them. How hard could he push her? "Your safe word will be *glowworm*."

She smiled softly at that, as he'd intended.

So he decided to trust his instincts, though the scheme swirling around his brain was either the best or worst idea he'd ever had. A smarter man would start slow and gradually introduce her to elements of his lifestyle. He leaned toward the ultimate test right off the bat. If she couldn't handle it, there was no sense in torturing them both with further outings to the clubroom.

"Help me, Tosin. What should I do? I don't like feeling clueless." She waited for him to take the reins. So he did.

"I'm only suggesting this because I think you're strong enough to handle it..." He hesitated. Once the words were out of his mouth, he wouldn't be able to reclaim them.

She looked up at him expectantly.

"Let me conduct a little experiment. I want to fuck you on that." He pointed to the spanking bench.

At first she recoiled. "How could you? I told you—"

He shushed her then, wishing they were far enough along in their explorations for him to have been able to gag her, blindfold her, prove his point without letting her work herself into a darker place first. If he did this right, he could mitigate those memories.

Replacing them with something decidedly not terrifying or horrible.

He hoped.

"Exactly, Kahori. What better way to show you how different I am and how much pleasure you can take from this place if you let go of the past?" He nuzzled her temple. "I know what I'm asking of you is difficult. Feel free to use your safe word, now or at any time. It won't change how I feel for you."

But this could destroy the budding love she had for him. Might have already done the damage like a late spring frost.

"May I see it first?" Kahori asked, a natural.

He led her to the apparatus and let her explore. Though she seemed wary at first, by the time she ran her hands over the custom-built frame and the deeply padded surface covered in the softest leather, she nodded.

"This seems much more comfortable than the one they had at the place I went to." She surprised him then with her bravery and daring. "Would you tie me to it? So that I don't freak out and fall?"

She couldn't know that bondage was his favorite aspect of BDSM.

It was just another way they were ultimately compatible.

"Of course." He kissed her gently. "But why stop there? I think I'll spank your perfect ass before we get to the good stuff." Kahori shuffled before him. He smirked. "Something wrong?"

She shook her head.

"Getting horny thinking of me having my way with you, and bringing you even more pleasure than last night while I do it?" He leaned in closer, whispering the suggestion so that she had to concentrate only on him and what he was doing to her.

Kahori nodded.

Tosin's hand flashed out, burying in her hair. She didn't flinch, not even when he fisted the strands then used them to tip her head back slightly. Instead, her lips parted and her cheeks flushed.

There was no doubt—she was made for this.

"I want to hear you answer me. Say, 'yes, sir,'" he commanded.

When the words rolled off her tongue, they were the sweetest thing he'd ever heard.

Tosin rewarded her appropriately. He kissed her until neither one of them could breathe. At the same time he unwound her fresh *pareu* from her body and dropped it to the floor. It was handy for quick disrobing. His new favorite garment. If she wasn't strutting around this place naked while they were at sea, he hoped she'd always wear one of those.

He froze. She'd never said she was coming with them. They hadn't discussed it since the disastrous end of their cave sex.

"Did I do something wrong?" she asked.

"No." Tosin rubbed the tip of his nose against hers. "You're perfect."

Refocusing, he lifted her onto the spanking bench then withdrew a set of silk ties from the drawer at the base. It didn't take long to have her secured to the equipment.

Kahori tested her bonds, unable to budge, never mind break free.

To be absolutely sure she wouldn't get carried away and injure herself later, he landed a single stinging swat on her ass.

She yelped and jerked but didn't budge. So he ran his finger down her crack then slipped a single finger into her pussy. It didn't surprise him in the least to find her soaked.

It did relieve him, though. He licked her slickness from his hand after he withdrew.

Perfect.

Though ordinarily he would take pride in teasing her for hours, today he planned to lean toward simple and to the point. The one where she couldn't deny how hard she came for him in these conditions. That was all he needed to show her today. The rest could follow later.

Tosin ran his hands all over her body, making sure there were no uncomfortable contact points, especially considering her lingering bruises. Another reason to keep things short and sweet.

He spoke to her the entire time he admired her body, assessed the right way to make his point. And when he was satisfied, he ripped off his bathing trunks then mounted the table and her.

His cock was painfully hard. It rested between her cheeks, making him long to claim her ass as well as her pussy. Some other time.

Tapping the head against her clit, he realized he'd nearly forgotten a condom.

Kahori groaned when he retrieved one from a fishbowl on a table nearby. "Tosin?"

"Yes?" He caressed the length of her back as he repositioned himself.

"When you come, will you..."

"Ask for anything you want, Kahori. I'm here to make your dreams come true." He kissed her shoulder blade as he notched his cock in her hungry pussy.

"Will you pull out and come on me instead of in that rubber?" She couldn't move much, but she squirmed within her confines. "I want to feel your passion for me."

"Fuck yes." He couldn't stop himself then from pressing into her, though he tried to go as slowly as his libido would allow. "See how much deeper it feels this way?"

"Mmmm..." She didn't object.

"You're okay, right?" He reached forward and cupped her neck in his palm, getting her attention. He should have put a mirror in front of her so he could monitor her expression. Based on her moan, this would work just fine for now, though.

"Yes, sir."

"Good girl." He beamed as he began to ride her, making sure to grind his pelvis into hers so that her clit stroked the ridge of the spanking bench just so.

Tosin withdrew his cock completely then reintroduced it to her, sliding deeper until his balls tucked tight against her ass. He did this repeatedly, fucking her with the entire length of his dick. It didn't take long before she was rocking back against him and calling out his name.

"What would you like, Kahori?" he asked, though he already knew the answer.

"I want to come. Then feel you coming on me. I want to know you feel this too," she admitted.

"I do." He leaned forward, blanketing her even as he began to drive into her body faster and harder. If he'd thought she was responsive the night before, it was nothing compared to the way she unraveled then.

Her pussy milked his cock, tugging on it even as she prepared to shatter.

When he realized she couldn't hold out a moment longer, he murmured, "Go ahead, come for me. Come on me, Kahori. Prove to us both that when we're together, that's all that matters. Feel how much better it is when you come like this. Give everything to me. And know that you have all of me in return."

Kahori screamed his name as she came. Spasms racked her for so long he thought she might pass out. Instead, she shouted, "Please, Tosin, now! I want to feel it!"

How could he resist an invitation like that?

He couldn't.

Tosin pulled out of her pussy, mourning the loss of juicy pressure on his shaft. Then he stripped off the condom. It only took a couple of powerful tugs before come rushed from his balls out the tip of his shaft. He painted Kahori with his release, making sure every last drop splashed onto her back and ass.

And when he'd emptied his balls, he used his trunks to dry her off before untying her and wrapping her in her *pareu*. She floated, not quite seeing anything clearly, it seemed. So he let her enjoy the high while he took care of business.

He'd already lifted her into his arms and looked down into her rosy face when she smiled up at him and tipped her face toward him for a kiss. He obliged her request.

"What did you think?" he asked softly. He knew how her body voted on the experience, but what about her mind?

"I think I want to do it again. Soon." She smiled sheepishly. "Can we do that?"

He laughed. "Give me ten minutes, then I'll be happy to show you around."

As it turned out, they didn't leave until Kahori's stomach growled and he realized he needed to take care of all her needs, not just the sexual ones.

Tosin threw on his shorts and wrapped her up again before carrying her toward his room. *Their* room. Whether she stayed or not, it would never belong to anyone else. "I love you, Kahori."

"I love you too, Tosin," she murmured groggily.

Of course, on the way to his quarters, they seemed to pass everyone else. What were they all doing in their cabins in the middle of the day anyway?

Waverly and Archer gave them a thumbs-up as they headed toward the lunch buffet. Sabine and Miguel teased him about the hickey Kahori had marked him with at some point. He didn't care. He wore the thing like a medal of honor.

And when Marta slipped out of Banks's room, she tossed Kahori a wink.

"I'm surprised the whole ship isn't rocking by now!" Tosin shouted with a laugh.

At that, Dr. Kleveno poked her head out of Captain Alex's room and said, "We're working on it. Now shut up and go away, would you, loudmouth?"

Kahori and Tosin cracked up as they fell into his bed and ordered room service. He didn't want to let her out of his sight even long enough to inhale a meal upstairs. He'd much rather eat her while they waited for the main course.

She had no objections.

∾ TWENTY ∾

A few days later Kahori paced the lobby of her uncle's resort. Even the gorgeous views of the overwater cabins and the lagoon beyond couldn't calm her any longer. Behind her Miguel and Sabine were signing the contracts that would establish one of the grow domes for their priceless cancer-fighting algae right here on Uncle Kimo's *motu*. After meeting the guys and seeing how they looked out for her, he'd changed his mind about getting involved in their project. And that was even before he'd seen Sabine's demonstration of how her developing formula destroyed cancer cells.

While it should have been a day of celebrations, shared prosperity, and pride that her often overlooked country could become such an important part of bettering the entire world, her father's absence was even more pronounced than it had been as she'd passed the time hoping for his return while on the *Divemaster.*

Steadying hands came to rest on her shoulders, keeping her from making another circuit of the open-air gathering place. Tosin asked, "How can I help?"

Those four simple words, so full of empathy and kindness, nearly had her bawling.

She spun around and plastered herself to him. Sheltering arms enfolded her in his warmth.

"Pāpā isn't coming back." She finally admitted it to herself. "Not ever. He's gone."

"Don't give up, Kahori." He squeezed her. "We're going to keep looking."

Shaking her head, she insisted, "He would never have left me. Not after my mother—"

Sniffling, she tried to hold herself together. Too late, she realized the conversation had ceased.

Miguel and Sabine were watching her worriedly, while Uncle Kimo joined her and Tosin.

"I want to say you're wrong." Uncle Kimo ran his knuckles over her cheek, collecting her tears. "But I feel the same. He would never have betrayed you. He's not involved in this scam. But I bet he figured out who was. He always was the smartest one in the family."

Kahori lost it at that. She sobbed, clinging to Tosin.

He rocked her, promising to help her search for answers, if not her father himself. Nothing could console her. Snot and tears leaked from her despite her best attempts to bottle it up inside again.

Kimo wandered to the reception desk where Hemi usually greeted their guests. He opened a drawer and rummaged toward the back, muttering about tissues. Instead, he froze, as if he'd laid his hand on a scorpion instead.

"What's wrong?" Banks asked.

Uncle Kimo's face twisted in disbelief as he withdrew a velvet pouch. One Kahori recognized from her workshop. When he looked inside, he cursed. Next, he took a wad of cash that would easily cover several years' worth of the resort's operations from the hiding spot, along with a passport. A plane ticket was jammed inside. When he flipped the book open to the photo page, he roared. "HEMI!"

"Yeah?" Her cousin—who might as well have been her brother—stuck his head around the corner as if the sound that had just ripped from his father's chest at the proof of his betrayal and imminent departure was something he heard all the time. The noise was one Kahori would never forget.

It echoed her own pain and terror.

"You?" Uncle Kimo's clay-colored skin shed its vibrancy. Ashen, he stared at his son. Then he threw the damning evidence at him. Pearls skittered across the floor, bouncing everywhere. "Tell me this is not what it looks like. No son of mine could be this rotten inside. He couldn't do this to another human being, never mind his own family. Hemi! Tell me!"

Kahori quivered in Tosin's hold, only staying upright thanks to his arms banded around her.

Instead, Hemi drew a long bone-handled knife from a sheath on his belt.

"I never meant for it to come to this." He stopped short of apologizing. "I only wanted to make enough extra money to get the hell off this island. Have a real life in a modern city. But...things got out of control. Once I'd earned what I needed, my partners wouldn't let me stop, let me go. I was still just as trapped as ever in this ass-end of the Earth. And now that I'm an hour from leaving, you won't stop me. No one will. I'm finally going to be free."

"You could have been honest!" Kimo's face gained all its color back and then some. He looked nearly burgundy as rage and disbelief brewed within him. "I would have helped you achieve your dreams. Here or elsewhere."

"Good. That's what I want from you now. Let me go. Let me leave." Hemi inched toward the exit.

"Where is my brother?" The frosty calm with which Uncle Kimo asked the question lodged in Kahori's throat terrified her. She didn't want to hear the answer she already knew in her heart.

Hemi didn't answer. He stared out at the ocean beyond the lagoon.

"What did you do?" Kimo stepped forward. Then again.

"*I* didn't do anything!" Hemi waved his hands in front of him as if he was completely innocent. "Uncle Ruru got too nosy, taking those packages to the airport. He noticed that I'd opened and resealed them all. Figured out that I'd swapped the pearls for fakes. Really amazing fakes. Stupid *papa'a* would never know the difference. Hell, even my partners didn't realize I'd started swapping out fakes for the 'real' stolen merch I was passing on to them for a little while. I guess they weren't quite as stupid as Kahori's other customers, though, since they showed up here. I'd almost gotten away. And now I will. Finally. Thanks for chasing them off for me, Tosin, so that I had time to finalize my travel plans and set up a place to go from here where no one will ever find me."

"Hemi," Uncle Kimo growled in warning. He looked as dangerous as their ancestors when fighting a rival tribe.

"When they went after Kahori, assuming she was in on the double-cross, I ran to her house. I wanted to clean up that one last package I couldn't find earlier in the evening and any other evidence. I didn't want them snapping my neck. You don't know them and what they're capable of."

"Yes, I do," Kahori whispered.

Her agony was enough to cut through the father and son's argument. They both looked at her, with various degrees of dismay and lament.

"I never meant for you to get hurt," Hemi swore. "Uncle Ruru either." He balked then. "But he came straight to Kahori's when he heard her scream. Thought she might be on her way there. Or maybe he followed me since he knew what I'd gotten tangled up in. Uncle Ruru came for me. Out of his mind. I told him I'd split the profits. He went crazy. Told me that if anything had happened to Kahori, I would pay. He charged me. It was reflex. Instinct."

He looked at the knife in his hand.

"What did you do, Hemi?" Uncle Kimo dropped to his knees.

"I only tried to defend myself." He swallowed hard. "I never meant to kill him."

Kimo threw his head back and unleashed a wail that Kahori felt straight to the core of her soul. She accompanied him with a scream of her own that made a ghastly duet. Her body thrashed in Tosin's hold, but he wasn't letting her out of his grip, away from the madness unfolding across the room.

"You're not going to let me go." Hemi wasn't asking.

His father snarled, then sealed their fates. "No. You're going to confess to the council and accept your punishment."

"I can't do that." Hemi shook his head.

Archer, Miguel, and Banks rose, stalking closer to Hemi.

They were nowhere close enough to stop him from charging, knife raised, toward his own father.

Uncle Kimo closed his eyes for the barest of moments then swiped his arm out, beneath his desk. When he raised it again, his spear gun pointed straight at Hemi's black heart.

He didn't stop.

Kimo pulled the trigger, launching a harpoon through the chest of his only offspring. He'd always prided himself on clean, quick kills when he provided for his family from the fruit of the island's life. This time was no different.

Hemi staggered one more step then fell, face-first, onto the floor, already gone.

Uncle Kimo knelt beside the corpse. He spoke in his native tongue, offering a prayer and a plea to the gods for *utu*.

"What is he doing?" Tosin whispered in her ear.

"Seeking balance." She sniffled. "He's asking for *mana* to restore our family's honor. Sort of like karma in other cultures. Trying to erase Hemi's sins and protect us from any lasting effects of them."

Tosin may not have understood or believed as the elders from her village did, but he respected her uncle's values and let the man do whatever it took to process his betrayal, grief, and loss.

Kahori wondered then what her father would think of Tosin standing strong beside her, propping her up on the hardest day of her life, and if Uncle Kimo's sacrifice would appease his spirit.

A single clap of thunder boomed out over the clear, sunny day. It rattled the windows and lasted for so long that everyone stood and examined the sky for a rogue cloud.

There were none.

"I love you too, Pāpā." Kahori kissed her fingers then held them to the sky. "Goodbye."

TWENTY-ONE

Kahori stood on the deck of the *Divemaster* a few days later. It had taken a while to wrap up the legalities surrounding her father's and Hemi's deaths to the satisfaction of both the Cook Islands Ministry of Justice and the tribal elders.

Tosin took her hand in his and kissed it softly before surprising her by reaching into his pocket and withdrawing something she recognized immediately. "I want you to wear this, and think of me."

He fastened the leather around her wrist before placing his palm flat against hers so that their complementary bracelets aligned perfectly for a moment, just as she had designed.

Never had she thought she would be the lucky person to share a bond—or the symbol of it—like this.

"Where will you be going?" she asked.

"I'm not sure." He shrugged as if he didn't care anymore either. "In fact, I was kind of thinking I might stay a while. There's a clause in my contract with Archer that says I can sell my share to him if I ever want out."

She couldn't keep silent then. "No! That would be such a waste!"

Tosin spun around, away from her. "I understand if you don't feel the same way I do…"

Kahori covered her mouth with her hand before reaching for him. With gentle pressure on his shoulder she attempted to turn him to face her again. "That's not how I meant it. It's just that I've already decided…if your offer from the glowworm cavern still stands…"

He whipped around to stare at her, seeming to hold his breath as he waited for her to finish her sentence.

"I'd like to come with you."

"Are you sure?" He rushed to close the gap between them then, nearly crushing her in a hug worthy of all eight of an octopus's arms.

She nodded. "Yeah. To be honest, I don't think I can ever call this place home again. There are too many bad memories. Pāpā—"

Her voice cracked. Tosin rocked her gently until she could continue.

"He was the reason I stayed as long as I did. I love it here, don't get me wrong, but it was holding back my career—and my ability to live my life to the fullest. With you, everything is possible. You've shown me that every day that we've spent together. There are so many things I regret not telling my *pāpā*. About how important he was to me and how I stayed because of him. I don't want to screw that up again. I love you, Tosin. I won't ever forget to show you how much."

"I promise I'll keep proving my love to you, too." He lifted her chin so he could stare into her eyes when he swore, "I'll make you so fucking happy that you never get homesick. And if you do, well, I do happen to have a private jet at my disposal. Just saying."

Kahori laughed. "Good to know."

Just then Banks and Marta wandered over wearing matching grins. "I didn't mean to eavesdrop, dear." Marta squirmed in between her and Tosin to hug her. "But did you say you're staying?"

Kahori nodded, tears welling in her eyes. How had she gotten lucky enough to find the man of her dreams and extend her family all at once when she needed them most?

Tosin squeezed her then teased Marta. "Why does that sound like you might be joining us for an extended visit yourself?"

"I guess there's something about this boat. It sucks you in and you can never leave." She beamed up at Banks. "Or maybe it's the abundance of sexy men onboard that tempt us women to become permanent cruisers."

"Arrrrgh, I can agree with that." Sabine did her best—really awful—pirate imitation as she joined them.

Miguel, Archer, Waverly, and Captain Alex came to see what all the fuss was about.

"Did I hear we've got ourselves a new permanent cruiser?" Captain Alex asked warmly. When Kahori nodded, he squished her in a one-armed hug.

"You know, now that Kimo signed on to add a grow dome to his *motu*, we'll probably be making

Aitutaki part of our regular rounds." Miguel shared the good news. She wondered if he'd been keeping it in his back pocket in case he needed to persuade her not to break Tosin's heart.

As if she could do that without also crushing her own.

Kahori looked around at the smiling faces that surrounded her with love, companionship, friendship, inspiration, support, and parental-esque advice. As sunset began to light the sky on fire, she couldn't imagine a more perfect way to finish one phase of her life and welcome in another. "Thank you all for making this the easiest decision of my life. Despite everything that's happened, and how quickly things changed, I'm sure that this is where I belong. With you. I hope you don't mind if I say I love you all. I'll be forever grateful to Banks and Archer, and the rest of you, for making this special project a reality."

Archer ruffled her hair as if she was his beloved little sister.

And when he turned around, Kahori noticed a sheen in Waverly's eyes. Pride in her boyfriend overwhelmed her. "She's right, Archer. Without you— without what you've built—we'd all still be lost."

He cleared his throat as if searching for the right thing to say and faced Waverly. "You know, I didn't have very much to do with it. Banks deserves credit for both the brainstorming and the hard work that made the Divemaster Project and the Banks Foundation realities. But I have to say that I'm happier now than I've ever been in my life before and with you—everyone, but especially you, Waverly—by my side, each and every day will only get better. That's why..."

Archer reached into his pocket as he dropped to one knee in front of his soul mate and the rest of their makeshift family. Everyone gasped when he flipped open the lid of the jewelry box Kahori knew so well and exposed her creation to the final rays of the tropical sun.

The ring came alive, diamonds and fire opals reflecting the light, which enhanced the luster of the magnificent—definitely genuine—black pearl nestled at its center.

It was the perfect thing, at the perfect time, for the perfect people.

Kahori was convinced.

This had been meant to be.

She leaned into Tosin as Archer said to Waverly, "...I'm begging you. Please, marry me."

The socialite turned badass military pilot squealed like a little girl then flung herself at her boyfriend. No, fiancé. He steadied her long enough to slip the ring on her finger.

It was a perfect match, and a perfect fit.

As everyone oohed and aahed over Kahori's handiwork, congratulations were passed all around.

"I have a feeling we may become wedding experts before too long." Captain Alex snorted. "I just have one question..."

"What?" Archer asked suspiciously.

"Can I be the flower girl?" Captain Alex propped one hand on his hip and flashed a silly smile.

Though they laughed at the time, none of the guys let him back out of his commitment down the road.

And he made the prettiest flower girl ever. All four times he filled the role before taking Dr. Kleveno for a walk down the aisle.

ABOUT THE AUTHOR

Jayne Rylon is a *New York Times* and *USA Today* bestselling author. She received the 2011 RomanticTimes Reviewers' Choice Award for Best Indie Erotic Romance.

Her stories used to begin as daydreams in seemingly endless business meetings, but now she is a full-time author, who employs the skills she learned from her straight-laced corporate existence in the business of writing. She lives in Ohio with two cats and her husband, the infamous Mr. Rylon.

When she can escape her purple office, Jayne loves to travel the world, SCUBA dive, take pictures, avoid speeding tickets in her beloved Sky and—of course—read.